what's
LEFT *of* US

what's
LEFT *of* US

AMANDA MAXLYN

ISBN-13:978-0692322772
ISBN-10:0692322779

Editing provided by: Jennifer Roberts-Hall and Rebecca Peters- Golden
Cover design provided by: Mae I Design and Photography

Interior designed and formatted by Tara Jones with:

www.emtippettsbookdesigns.com

what's LEFT *of* US
Table of Contents

~℃ ℃~

For my boys.
You two have taught me that any fear is worth facing.
I love you to the stars and back.

"You gain strength, courage, and confidence by every experience in which you really stop to look fear in the face. You must do the thing which you think you cannot do."

— Eleanor Roosevelt

Author's Note

I believe there are obstacles in life that we must face and overcome before we are given our happily ever after. Parker and Aundrea are no different when it comes to making their dreams come true.

I hope you enjoy this next chapter of their life together as they work on overcoming their deepest fears in order to have their honest and heartwarming conclusion.

This book is because of you, the reader. Thank you for wanting more just as much as I wanted to give it to you.

With love,
Amanda
xox

PROLOGUE

Aundrea

Fear. It's all around us. It finds a way inside, lodging deep within, refusing to surrender. It latches on, following you on this path called life. The way it makes our bodies tremble through our core, perspire with one thought, or makes our hearts feel as if they're coming to a standstill, causing all blood flow to rush from our head to our toes. It's the one word that can instantly cause our breathing to become slow and labored, stirring up the worst emotions within.

Suddenly my chest becomes too tight to bear. My legs go numb and my arms feel weak. My heart is beating too fast and, no matter how much I pray for it to slow, and the tight pain to go away, it doesn't.

I'm gasping for air. "My chest. It's too tight." I claw at my shirt, as if I could rip it off. The once soft fabric now feels like fire, burning away my flesh.

"Mom, I don't think she's okay!"

"Aundrea?!"

"I can't breathe. My ... tight … the pain … it won't stop. I can't feel my arms, or …" Oh my God, this is it.

I fall to my knees.

"Is she having a heart attack?" Panicky, Genna stands

and yells for my dad.

Every dream I've had, every sense of hope—everything I've feared is burning them away right before my eyes.

Death.

It's easy to forget what matters most when you're distracted by your deepest fear, which, in my case, is leaving behind everyone I cherish most. Sometimes it's the most disturbing thoughts that tunnel their way to your core and hold on, no matter how hard you try to shake them.

The afterlife doesn't scare me. The unknown can be magical when you really think about it. The beauty of possibility.

There are muffled voices around me, yelling and screaming, but my eyes are frozen. I can't move my head to see who's speaking. I can't even be certain where I am at the moment.

I begin to feel like I'm floating and it's then that I realize I'm being put on a stretcher. There are two men yelling. *Why are they yelling? Are they yelling at me?*

A cold rush of air startles me as a mask is put over my face. It's the first time I get a deep, fulfilling breath since this all started.

"You're going to be okay. Keep your eyes open for me, okay?" one of the men instructs, leaning close to my face.

I try to nod, but he shakes his head. "Don't try to move." I go cold, every limb gone numb. Then, pain.

I don't think I've ever felt so much pain in all my life. It's as if a hundred men are standing on top of me, stabbing my chest with razor-sharp knives. I swear, with each jab of pain I can hear the crack of the blades stabbing deeper inside of me, slowly ripping me apart. Then the pain pierces my heart and I cry out.

"Someone needs to call Parker!" Genna screams.

The men start running and I feel like I'm flying. The wind washes over me and it's almost calming.

My surroundings go blurry as I'm lifted. Everything is happening so fast. My shirt is ripped open and freezing stickers are placed on my chest.

Cries fill my ears, drowning out the loud banging from the men moving around. I don't know where I am, but when I hear my mom say, "Parker, its Aundrea. We're going to the hospital," I let my eyes drift closed and just pray the pain will stop. And that Parker will get to me before it's too late.

chapter ONE

Aundrea

Three Months Earlier

The future.

It's terrifying to think about.

Sometimes life can be run by our emotions; how we feel about ourselves can dictate the path our life takes.

Before Parker entered my life, I didn't think about tomorrow, much less my future. But he changed me. The day he told me he could see my future was the day I knew I would stop at nothing to make sure I saw the start and end of each day. For him.

For us. It's when *our* future began.

"Aundrea?" a gentle voice asks, breaking me from my thoughts. I shiver as Parker grasps my hand, helping me. My senses are heightened, trying to glean some clue as to where we are.

"Can I look now?" I giggle, nearly tripping over the uneven ground. The blindfold Parker had me put on before leaving our apartment slips a little as I catch my balance, but it doesn't fall off.

His grip on my arm tightens as he chuckles. "Almost. A

what's **LEFT** *of* **US**   **5**

couple more steps."

He guides me up a small set of steps, loosening his hold as we reach the top. He lets go of my arm, but doesn't say a word; only the sound of crickets fills the night air. A welcome breeze kisses my face softly.

My ears perk up at the sound of a key entering a lock. "Where are we?" I ask, even though I know he won't answer. I have a strong urge to just rip off the blindfold.

"We have one last tiny ledge to step over, so careful now." Holding my elbow, he leads me through the door. A few steps in, we stop abruptly. "Okay, open."

I pull down the blindfold and blink away blurriness as my eyes adjust.

"What is this?" I stand, breathless, taking in my surroundings. Before me is a large open layout of living space leading into what a glimpse suggests is a kitchen. I look down, shuffling my feet. I'm standing on dark, rich hardwood floors that run into the most beautiful, detailed floor molding I have ever seen. To my side is a large, wide staircase leading to an open space that overlooks where we're standing.

Of course, I know what this is — a *house* — so my question should really be, "Why are we here?"

Parker steps in front of me, taking one of my hands in his. I look up, meeting my husband's crystal blue eyes.

"Do you know that paper is the traditional one year anniversary gift?" I shake my head, bemused. Handing me a folded note, he says quietly, "Open it."

I fumble with the paper. I suck in a sharp breath as I read the deed I'm clenching in clammy fingers. "Parker, you bought us a house." It doesn't come out as a question, but rather a stunned statement.

His throat bobs as he rubs the back of his neck nervously, and a light sheen of sweat forms on his forehead. I smile at his nervousness, which causes his shoulders to relax.

"Aundrea, I was taught that when you find the person you're meant to be with, you should do everything in your power to keep them. Spend every day of your life proving to them that they're worth it. You're always by my side, helping me, wanting to protect me, and showing me that I can be the best man possible. Together, we've started to build a life that means something to us, and I want the next chapter of it to start here."

He motions at the house around us. "I want to grow old, have lots of children, and hear their little footsteps run around on these hardwood floors. I want to have a future with you in this house."

I cover my mouth to stop my lip from quivering. "I love it," I mumble, my voice barely audible. I haven't even stepped more than a foot into the place, but I can already tell by the hardwood floors and open layout that I'm going to fall head over heels for this house.

"You do?"

I look around the room, taking in the stone fireplace, high ceiling, bright lights, and crown molding. "It's absolutely gorgeous."

"Like you."

Heat rises to my cheeks and I'm almost certain my ears have turned bright red. We've been together for three years now, and been married for one year, and this man can still make me blush.

"Come here." He takes my hand, lacing our fingers together. "Let me show you around *our* place."

I give a small nod, allowing him to lead the way. He takes me through the house, showing me the den, the living area, every bedroom and closet. Each room seems larger and more extravagant than the last. I'm surprised by how large this house is. It's more than I could have ever dreamed. Parker explains that it's a newly built house, which is why the walls are so plain, which I don't mind because we'll be able to add our Mr. and Mrs. Jackson touches to it.

Parker shows me every corner, ending with us standing in front of a sliding glass door off the dining room. A cool blast of air hits me as I follow him out to the large deck.

"Parker," I breathe. My mouth drops open at the sight before me. The deck is covered with glowing candles and, in the center, a blanket is laid out with a bottle of champagne and two glasses.

"It's amazing, huh?" he asks, motioning to the large backyard.

"It's perfect." I'm in absolute awe as I realize this is all ours.

Coming up behind me, Parker wraps his arms around my waist, pulling me against his chest. "We're far enough away from the city that you can stargaze as much as you want with no light pollution."

Resting my head on his shoulder, I look up at the black sky. I could stare at this view all night. I fill my lungs with the cool night air and let it out slowly as I take in our expansive back yard.

"Is this for real?" I ask half choked up, half smiling.

"Very much. Our future continues *here*, Aundrea."

I turn to face him. "This place is amazing, Parker. Honestly, I couldn't have picked a better place for the two of us."

Engulfing me in his arms, he hugs me tightly, kissing the top of my head.

Snuggling in closer, I start thinking about the last couple months. How could he have managed this without my finding out?

"How did you do this?"

"What do you mean?"

I laugh. "How did you purchase a house without me knowing? I mean, I understand I've been busy with finals and gearing up for graduation next month, but I didn't think I was *that* out of it."

"I know the realtor." He shrugs with a half smile. "He brings his dog into the clinic. Three months ago he mentioned this property and when I saw him again recently he brought it back up, surprised it was still on the market. I knew I had to see it and, when I did, I couldn't resist. The price was right and the rest, as they say, is history."

Of course he'd know the realtor.

I laugh again and Parker raises an eyebrow. "What's so funny?"

"What if I'd hated the house?"

"I knew you wouldn't."

"Confident are you?"

"When it comes to you, yes."

Giving him a warm smile, I wrap my arms back around his hard body, resting my head on his chest. "Here," he says, pulling me to the center of the deck where the candles are glowing softly.

Settling under the blanket, I snuggle against him, looking up at the clear sky and the stars shining above us. I can imagine myself stargazing out here every night, or snuggling on a chaise longue with my Kindle and a glass of white wine.

This is our home.

Parker reaches for the champagne bottle, so I wiggle forward to give him more room. He pops the cork and pours us each a glass, not allowing the bubbles to overflow.

"Happy wedding anniversary, Aundrea. Here's to many more." He raises his glass and I do the same.

"Happy anniversary, handsome."

The bubbles tickle my throat as I take a small sip, watching my husband do the same.

There isn't a day that goes by that I'm not thankful for this man before me and all his surprises. Over the last three years he's done nothing but be supportive in all I do, constantly trying to give me everything that I deserve. He's taught me to embrace life, and I can't wait to welcome whatever life decides to throw our way next.

~℃ ℈~

"Wait. Stop a minute and back up. He bought you a house? Like, a *house* house?" my best friend Jean screams into my ear the following evening. *A* house *house? Is there any other kind?*

Moving the phone away in an attempt to get my hearing back, I answer, "Yes, he bought *us* a house. Not just me."

"Same thing." *Um ... okay?* "Damn, Dre." I can picture her sitting on the couch in her Minneapolis apartment shaking her head in awe as she speaks. "When's the move? Did you have any idea he was even looking?"

I shrug, even though she can't see me. "We're not sure on a move-in date, but since our lease is up at the end of next month, we're hoping soon. Parker said the realtor doesn't think it will be a problem. The loan has already gone through, so we'll just need an inspection for the final okay. And, no, I had no idea he was looking. It just sort of fell in his lap."

"Shit. I can't believe that man sometimes."

Neither can I. "I know."

"The timing will be perfect, too. Take your last final, graduate, and move into that big new house of yours. You're finally entering the real world!" The shuffling sounds on Jean's end suggest she's getting more comfortable. "If it weren't for me, the two of you wouldn't even be together."

"That's not true!"

"Sure it is. I practically had to force you to go home with him that night at Max's Bar. If it weren't for me, you would never have left with him, there'd be no ring on that pretty little finger of yours, and there definitely wouldn't be any house. So, you're welcome."

"Thanks." It comes out flat, but I pick the tone back up. "For the record, I went home with him all on my own." She giggles. "Are you coming to Rochester this weekend?" I ask, changing the subject.

"I think so. It all depends on Kevin. He mentioned something about needing to pick up a shift for Jason."

Kevin is another veterinarian Jason met in college and introduced to Parker when he moved here. They asked him to join the practice a little over a year ago, and recently he became the third partner at the clinic. He also happens to be Jean's boyfriend—not that she approves of that word.

"Well, if not, maybe I can come up for the day or something?"

"I'd like that, Dre. It's been forever."

"It's been two weeks!"

"My point. Forever."

I smile just as I hear keys fumbling in the door. "Hey, Parker's home. I'll chat with you later, okay?"

"Fine, go hang out with that man candy of yours while I sit here in my empty apartment watching reruns of *Gossip Girl*."

I chuckle, ending the call as Parker enters our apartment.

Standing in the entryway in gray dress slacks and a black button-down shirt unbuttoned a little at the top, he looks just as good as he did this morning when he left for work. His blond hair is disheveled, as if he's run his hand through it a hundred times, suggesting a stressful day.

"What's all the laughing about?"

"Jean."

"Ah." He raises his eyebrows and smiles.

Setting his keys in the dish by the door, he walks into the living room and sits next to me, pushing my physics book aside. It falls to the floor as his lips meet mine, gentle and soft. He takes my top lip into his mouth and tenderly kisses it.

Leaning back, he gives me a wink. "Hi."

"Hello, handsome." I run my fingers along his stubbled cheeks, smiling. "How was your day?"

His shoulders relax as he sinks into the couch. "Busy, but good. Yours?"

I groan, throwing my head back playfully. "Studying. Lots and lots of studying. I don't think I can see straight. Change of subject, please."

He laughs, pulling me in for another kiss. "That bad, huh?"

"I'm just anxious for my last final to be over."

The moment I was cleared of needing further cancer treatment, I sunk all my spare time—plus some—into my studies. I doubled up on course work, taking as many classes as I could so that I could graduate in a timely manner. There were semesters my family—including Parker—thought I was crazy to take on so many sleepless nights and long study hours, but I looked at it as making up for missed opportunities, and I've truthfully enjoyed every second of it. I've worked so hard to get to this point, and the thought of graduating next month from the Winona State University, Rochester with a bachelor's in physics is the most rewarding and liberating feeling ever.

Parker winks, then stands and moves through the kitchen effortlessly, opening the fridge and taking out a beer. He looks over his shoulder at me, raising an eyebrow, and I nod.

He rejoins me on the couch and I use my shirt to twist the cap off my beer.

"No studying tonight, beautiful. We're celebrating."

I take a small, appreciative sip. "Celebrating what?"

"Our future."

"I thought we did that last night?" I bite my lip, remembering our naughty evening.

"Oh, we definitely celebrated last night."

I blush. I shouldn't be bashful thinking or talking about having sex, but when it comes to sex with Parker … it's hard not to feel the heat.

He sets his beer down on the coffee table and his face turns serious. "I've been thinking—don't give me that look, Aundrea."

"What look?"

"The look that says, 'Oh, boy, here we go!'"

I laugh. "Sorry. It's just, last night you surprised me with a house. I'm not sure what can top that."

He takes a deep breath. "When Mark showed me the house, the first thing that popped into my head was how we'll have all this space to fill." I can see the tension in the small lines forming around his eyes.

"What are you saying?"

He runs his hand through his hair and swallows hard.

"Maybe it's time we think about adding to the Jackson family."

"Like a dog?" I raise an eyebrow. It's a joke, but one I hope eases the tension in his eyes.

"No." He gives me a weak smile. "What if we considered the idea of starting a family? I mean, it's probably not going to happen overnight, but I think it's time we discuss our options. Look into what's available for us."

I don't realize I'm holding my breath until I suddenly feel lightheaded. Forcing myself to breathe, I brace against the armrest. "You mean … you want us to have a baby?"

He nods. Before I can say anything, he reaches for my arms, almost as if he knows what my reaction will be: passing out.

I kind of feel as if I might.

A baby.

Are we ready to have a baby?

Am *I* ready to have a baby?

chapter TWO

Aundrea

"**W**hat … do … think … baby?"

I can see Parker's mouth moving, but I don't catch every word that comes out. My mind is foggy. One mention of the word baby and I've gone blank.

"Earth to Aundrea," Parker laughs, giving my arm a little shake.

"I'm sorry." I try and collect my thoughts before saying anything further — or, rather, something stupid.

He looks so hopeful with his big boyish grin and wide eyes gazing at me, waiting for my response.

"I … um, I …"

I wait for my brain to catch up with my mouth. I try to calm my breathing, but can't. My hands feel clammy and I can't feel my toes. My entire body has gone numb.

"I'm sorry, what?" I know what, but maybe I've mistaken. Maybe he really asked me what I thought of Peggy, the new librarian at our local library.

"I said, what do you think about having a b-a-b-y? Baby." My chest heaves with each second that passes without saying anything. "Aundrea, listen to me. I know what you're thinking." *He has no idea.* "We're in this together. It's you and me. No one else—only us."

"I don't know what to say." I'm stunned.

"Aundrea, these last three years everything has been fine."

He means my health.

I wasn't expecting this conversation right now. Having a baby is something I've always wanted, and I knew being with Parker meant that dream was possible. He's given me life again, and I want nothing more than to give him the same. Of course we've talked about kids, but we've talked about a lot of things over the last three years. We've shared every dream, hope, and fear, and have been each other's biggest supporter in all of it.

Parker's eyes soften. He takes my hands in his. "I want us to build our family. I believe we're ready to have a baby. I know we are. *You* are. There is *nothing* to be afraid of," he reassures me. "Your last appointment with Dr. Olson went so smoothly and so did your last heart scan. I want a baby with you, Aundrea." He takes a deep breath and lets it out before adding, "There is nothing more I want in life than to start a family with you. To live out our dreams together."

I nod, slowly processing his words. "Can I have some time to think about it?"

His face falls, but he quickly recovers. "Of course."

"I want this Parker. I do, I promise."

"But?"

"There are no buts. I assure you. I just ... Give me a little time, please." I need to collect all the thoughts that are swimming around inside my head right now.

"What has you spooked? Talk to me."

Everyone has that one fear. The one they can't shake, no matter what. Being a cancer survivor has made me a better woman—a stronger woman, even. My heart condition doesn't even scare me. If anything, I believe my heart is the strongest it's ever been. But being faced with one of your biggest fears, and the realization that you *are* living with an incurable condition that could take you away from your family in an instant … *that* scares me.

Leaving *them.*

"It's not only me I have to think about."

He nods, knowing exactly what I mean.

The steam covering the mirror distorts my face. With one stroke, I wipe a path to show hazel eyes, pink lips, and round, healthy cheeks. I drop my towel and study my reflection. My hips are wider than they were when I was sick, my stomach a little fuller, and my arms show a little muscle definition. The woman that stares back at me is healthier, thanks to the right diet from a nutritionist and a husband who gives her all the activity she can handle. The woman I'm looking at not only feels happy, but looks it too.

Pinning my wet hair back, I leave it to air dry in the beachy waves I like.

When my hair started to grow back after chemo, it was much lighter than the strawberry blonde it used to be: mostly blonde, with a few glints of red shining in the sunlight. It was also less curly.

Finding a pair of dark, thick tights and my favorite gray sweater dress, I quickly finish getting ready in our empty bedroom. Parker left for work earlier than normal for a staff meeting. He seemed a little cold and standoffish after our conversation last night, but he insisted he was fine and okay with giving me time to think about the idea of having a baby.

I unpin my hair, shake out the damp waves, and slip into my black boots. Putting on a bit of make-up, I glance in the mirror to give my final approval before grabbing my purse off the kitchen table. I take one last look around to make sure I have everything before heading to the clinic to volunteer.

At the Mayo Clinic, I give the security guard a quick nod as I pass him and step into the elevator. It's the same guy, each week. He seems friendly enough, even though we've never said more than a few words about the weather.

My boot heels click softly against the boring white tile of the Oncology floor. I like the way heels look, but I love my flats more, though I'd never say that around Jean. The woman wholeheartedly believes every woman should wear heels daily, no matter their height or what they're doing.

Casey, the receptionist, greets me with a smile over the shoulder of the man she's helping. She's beautiful, with olive skin and long, silky black hair with straight bangs that frame her heart-shaped face perfectly.

It took me a while to start volunteering my time here. Coming face to face with others battling cancer and seeing them so vulnerable was difficult. But then I met Amy, a volunteer and cancer survivor who taught me that it's about giving people hope; encouraging them to keep moving forward and be strong because there is an end to the disease and that end doesn't have to result in something terrible. Being here is not only inspiring, but rewarding.

In the employee lounge, I put my things in a locker and put on my red volunteer vest. I pick up the tray of juice and packaged gingerbread cookies, chuckling. I remember the volunteers passing these out when I was getting chemotherapy. As a patient, I never understood the need for it, because patients rarely accept them. Now, though, I see that it's an icebreaker — an easy way to strike up a conversation. I never force anyone to talk to me or share anything about their cancer that they don't want to. I just let them know I'm available in case they want to talk. That I know what it's like to try and protect your friends and family from what you're feeling.

In a few strides I'm in the treatment room, and I scan the patients, taking in the familiar faces. Amy's already here, but instead of wearing the red vest and assisting the patients, she's reading in a chair, wearing a plain gray T-shirt and jeans.

She's been a huge inspiration to me and I've grown to really trust and respect her. It's hard to find someone you connect with who also understands what you have been through. We've become so close, I don't know what I'd do without her. I still go to Jean, but Amy understands me on a different level.

"Hi, Dre!" Her face brightens as I approach. Bless her heart, she's always happy and smiling. I've never heard her complain.

"Hey, you. What are you doing sitting over here?"

She grins. "I have the day off."

"Day off? Do you usually come in on your day off?"

She laughs, eyes bright. "I had an appointment this morning for a lab draw. Brandon and Ethan ran across the street to get some coffee and a donut before we drop Ethan off at school."

I smile. "What are you reading?" I motion at her Nook, changing the topic to one of my favorites.

It's one I've never heard before. "I just started it while I wait for the boys to come back."

"How is it?" I ask, setting the tray down and taking the seat next to her.

"It's so good. I'm loving it. Friends turned lovers. I'm a sucker for that."

"I love those too."

She pulls down the edges of her blue knitted hat with a small white flower on the side, as if trying to disguise the wig she still wears. After Amy finished chemo about a year ago, her hair grew back frail and thin, making it difficult to grow out. She's been on multiple medications and has seen a few specialists to help, but so far nothing has worked.

"Enough about my book. Did you get the job?"

"I did!" I cheer. I recently finished a small internship program at Astrotek Incorporated. During my exit interview they told me about a position that was opening up in the fall, so I applied and was called in for an interview shortly after.

"That's awesome!"

"Thank you. Parker and I are pretty excited. It's great to already know the staff, so it won't be awkward being the new girl, and the department I'll be in works closely with

NASA." I tap my feet on the floor with excitement. I'd love to work for NASA someday, but I would need a PhD in Astrophysics to do what I'd want.

"Wow."

"I know. And my brother-in-law offered me my job back at For the Love of Paws for the summer. I'll still volunteer here one day a week with you, so that will be nice."

"It seems like everything is falling into place for you."

"It appears to be." I take a deep breath. I itch to tell her about last night, but hold off.

"How was your anniversary?"

I'm certain my smile can't get any wider at the mention of that word. "It was beyond wonderful." I don't hold back when I tell her about the house, down to the last detail. Still, she senses I'm withholding something.

She tilts her head and looks at me as if she's reading into my mind; her eyes dim just a little. "What is it?"

As I'm about to reply, she smiles broadly and I turn around to see Brandon and Ethan walking in behind me.

"Hi, Mom," Ethan says, beaming, practically falling onto Amy's too-skinny frame.

"Hey, buddy."

"Hi, Aundrea." Brandon gives me a polite wave and smile.

"Good morning." I take in Ethan's short stature and curly brown hair. "Hi, Ethan, how are you?"

His little shoulders bounce. "Good."

Amy pulls Ethan back into a tight hug.

"Are you ready?" Brandon asks, rubbing her arm.

She glances at her watch then back to Brandon. "Yep!"

"All right, I'll take Ethan to say hi to Casey while you two finish up."

"Can I take a cookie before I go?" Ethan asks, reaching for the tray with expectant eyes.

"Of course, buddy." I push the tray closer. "You better take a couple," I whisper, giving Amy a wink.

He gives me a devilish smirk and fills his hands. Amy

and I watch as the two men in her life walk away. Well, as one walks and the other skips. Ethan's six and is as nonstop as the Energizer bunny.

"He adores that lady," Amy says of Casey. "She's started babysitting so Brandon and I can have a date night once a week."

"Aw, that's really nice of her. You two need that."

"Ethan's taken a liking to her and I can't even begin to tell you how good it feels to find someone that he admires so much."

"I bet." We both watch as Ethan laughs at something Casey said. "He's a good kid, Amy. You must be proud."

"I'm beyond proud. I have the best and most supportive husband, a charming and energetic little boy, and I've been given the chance to be here with them. I'd say I'm pretty blessed."

"I'd say you are, too."

"You'll have all that too someday, Dre."

I can't think of a better time to mention what's been consuming me since last night. "Actually, speaking of that."

"What?" Her ears practically perk up.

"Last night Parker brought up the idea of us starting a family."

"Dre!" she screams, causing heads to turn our way, and I hear Brandon chuckle. "What? Really?"

"Yes," I whisper, pleading she take it down a notch.

"Being a mother is the best thing to have ever happened to me. You'll make a great mom, Dre. I know it."

"Thank you."

I take a few short breaths.

"What is it?"

Here it goes.

"Is it strange that getting the news my cancer was back, or that I was diagnosed with a life-long heart condition doesn't scare me, but having the most important person in my world share the news they want to have a baby with me does? It's not that I don't want a baby because I do. But …"

Amy purses her lips and nods in complete understanding. "I get it. Honestly, I do. It's a huge decision, and one that involves more than just you and Parker. Being frightened makes you human. Don't let normalcy scare you, Aundrea. It's one of the best gifts you could ever be given, aside from love, and I'll be the first to say I hope to see the day when you're holding your baby in your arms."

I give her an honest smile. That's just it. Making the decision to have a child means it's not only about me anymore. I would have another human being to protect and think about.

To live for.

"Mommy, can we go now?" Ethan comes running back over, almost falling into her lap again.

"Yes, honey, Mommy's coming right now. Why don't you and Daddy get a head start and I'll meet you in two minutes?"

"Okay!" He turns on his green ninja turtle sneakered toes and runs down the hall.

She turns her attention back to me, but not before giving Ethan a lingering glance. "Seriously, though, Aundrea, I haven't met one person, myself included, who didn't have a mini panic attack when they decided to have a baby or found out they were pregnant. Trust me when I tell you, you're not alone. No one is 100% ready to have a baby, and if they say they are, they're lying. When I found out I was pregnant with Ethan I was so full of nerves I started puking with the test still in my hands!"

We laugh.

Amy begins to stand, Nook in hand. "I'm going to give you some of the best advice I was ever given."

I nod. I'll take any advice she has for me at this point.

"Our past shapes our future, but don't plan your future around past hardships. A baby is going to take time, Aundrea. It won't happen overnight. Don't let this happy time freak you out. Don't let your fear hold you back. You're going to make an amazing mom. Embrace it. You and Parker will learn the joys of parenthood, and it will forever change you, for the better."

I stand, pulling her into a hug. "Thank you." She knows exactly what to say, exactly when I need to hear it.

"Anytime. Call me and we'll do coffee soon, okay?"

"You got it."

She walks away, and I watch the smiles on Brandon and Ethan's faces as she approaches them. Brandon wraps his arm around her tiny waist as Ethan bounces down the hall a few strides ahead.

Standing in a room surrounded by patients hooked up to chemo machines as I watch one of my closest friends leave happily with her family, it feels like my past is colliding with my future. Life is all about doing the unimaginable. It's about taking on new challenges to overcome.

And I say, bring it on.

chapter THREE

Aundrea

It wasn't long after I finished chemo that I moved in with Parker. We never exactly talked about it; it just sort of happened. My things slowly showed up at his place, one by one. Then, one night when we were making dinner, I asked, "What do you think of the idea of me moving in?" and he only replied, "I thought you already did," followed by a wink. We haven't spent a night apart since.

Opening the apartment door, I call for Parker. "Anybody home?"

"In the kitchen."

Cupboard doors slam and he grunts. "You okay?"

"Yeah." He laughs. "Just fighting with the cabinets."

I'm happy, yet anxious to talk to him about the baby idea. To tell him I want to get started with the process as soon as we can.

I round the corner hurriedly, startling Parker.

"Sorry!" I shriek, freezing in place.

"I wasn't expecting you to come up behind be." He laughs, placing one hand over his heart. His head dips down then back up again showing his overly large smile.

I smile. "I've been anxious to see you all day."

His ears perk and his eyes become sultry as he gazes at me. "Is that so?" In a few short strides he's standing in front of me.

A tiny giggle slips through as I teasingly swat his shoulder. "Not in the way you're thinking."

I watch as Parker takes a step back and leans against the counter, posture relaxed. "Enlighten me then." The corners of his mouth are upward in a sly grin.

"I've been thinking a lot today about us having a baby … I've been thinking about everything, quite honestly."

Letting out a small breath, Parker pushes himself off the counter. All playfulness has slipped away. "Listen, I didn't bring up having a baby to freak you out, and if you really want to wait, we'll wait. We'll wait for as long as you need or want to. When you're ready, I'll be here." He kisses the top of my head, rubbing small circles on my arm.

Swallowing, I look into his eyes. "I want to. I dream of our baby, Parker," I whisper. I'll never be able to carry my own child because of all the chemo I went through, but my eggs were frozen before I even started treatment at seventeen.

"Our baby," he repeats. A smile reforms on my face and he follows suit. "You want to have a baby with me. I love the sound of that."

My smile is so wide I can feel the tightness in my cheeks and jaw. "Yes. With everything inside of me, Parker, I want it. Like you said, there is nothing to worry about. I have an appointment in a couple months that will hopefully set my visits with Dr. Olson to every six months, and my heart *is* under control. I take my medication every day, my last two scans were clear, and my blood pressure is right on." My words come out as if I'm trying to reassure myself, which, in a way, I am.

Or am I reassuring us both?

I'm in good health. There is no need to worry.

About anything.

"And later on, who knows? Maybe after we use my eggs and we're ready for another baby we'll look into adoption."

I've always been open to the idea of adoption, especially since my sister Genna is adopted.

I can see the tenderness in Parker's eyes, see what he sees when he looks at me. The immense love he has for me.

For us.

"For the second time in my life you have made my heart stop. And for the second time in my life, you have made me the happiest man alive." His words are confident.

I'm pretty sure *my* heart just stopped. To be certain it's still beating I bring my hand to my chest and wait to feel the thumps. When I do, I smile. *This is real.* It's all real.

He takes my hand and tugs me to his chest, holding on for dear life. "I love you."

"I love you more," I whisper back.

⁓ ℗ ℘ ⁓

Over the next few days, we do a lot of research on finding a surrogate, but we quickly conclude that there aren't that many choices in our area. The Mayo Clinic in Rochester has a program, but we want something more personal, so we confine our search to small agencies in the Minneapolis and St. Paul area.

I push my laptop away, needing a break. At Parker's chuckle, I snap my head in his direction. He doesn't even look up from his laptop as he shakes his head at me.

"What?" I ask with a hint of my own laughter.

"You."

"What about me?" I tilt my head to the side. "Hmm?"

He looks up. "You're cute when you're frustrated."

"Picking the right agency to find the woman who will help bring our child into the world is extremely important. One I'm not going to take lightly."

He holds his hands up, grinning. "Hey, I agree. I just think it's sexy, that's all."

"Well, then, I better get frustrated more often."

He scoots his chair closer to mine. "Only if I'm the one

who gets to make you un-frustrated," he says slowly, and tiny chills spread through me. I love when his voice goes deep and sexy. That rasp drives me crazy.

"And how do you suppose you would do that?"

"I could think of a few ways …"

My eyes shift from his eyes to his mouth as he licks his lips. I love when he does that. As if he's preparing himself for me.

"Yeah?"

"Uh-huh."

He leans forward, joining his mouth with mine. My eyes close at the light impact. He starts the kiss out slow, only allowing me a small taste. When I can't take his taunting any longer, I slip the tip of my tongue between his lips. We linger and explore. I have to keep myself from falling into him by resting a hand on the table edge. I can sense Parker doing the same.

I moan when the connection is broken. He's watching me intently as he leans back in his chair.

"Why did you stop?"

"Because if I didn't, I was going to take you right here on the table."

I don't see why that's a problem. "I would let you."

He gives me a devious grin. "Later, I promise. We have some work to do if we want to find an agency to meet with in a couple weeks."

My last class is next week, so we agreed that the best time to set up meetings with the agencies we like would be after my last class and before my graduation in May.

"Okay, okay," I grumble. I'm not too happy to stop the make out session with my hot-as-hell husband to continue looking at a computer screen, but I will if it means getting what I want.

I go back to the search engine, but stop. "What if this doesn't work?"

"What do you mean?"

"Let's say we find an agency and they can't help us? Or

we find one, but we can't find a surrogate we like."

"We won't stop until it does work."

"And if it's more expensive than what we've been researching?"

"Aundrea, we have enough in savings for a down payment with an agency, plus some. We'll have to get the facts, of course, and all the numbers, but I'm sure we can work out some contract with payments or get a loan for what we can't cover on our own. Besides, from what we've researched, this could take months, even years. We'll just keep saving as much as we can."

"I just really want this to work out."

"It will."

Now that we've started actually talking about having a baby, it's all I can envision for us.

It's all I want.

"Do you think we should tell our families? I mean, I've already told Amy."

"I think telling our friends and families would be great. I'm not sure if we should tell your mom, though," Parker jokes.

The woman likes to talk. If we tell her our plans my entire hometown of Northridge will know within a day. Easily.

"You're probably right." I giggle. "Maybe close friends only, along with Genna and Jason, of course. And we tell our parents once we have some news to share?"

"That sounds good. No reason to get their hopes up yet."

"Agreed."

Parker goes back to researching, but I decide to take a break and read something else. Something more … pleasurable. I love nothing more than getting lost in a good story, connecting with the characters. I've always found it fascinating how authors can bring a world to life.

The refrigerator door closes for the fifth time and Parker says, "How about I order some pizza? I'm not sure I'm in the mood to cook."

"Sure!" I call back, not looking up from my Kindle. I'm

not really hungry and, honestly, I don't think I could eat right now even if I were. I'm that sucked in to my novel.

"Or maybe Chinese?"

"Sure."

"Are you even listening to me?"

"Sure."

"In that case, what about a cock sandwich?"

"Really, handsome, anything."

His loud laugh fills the room. "What happened? What's funny?"

"You." His grin is anything but playful; it's … naughty.

"What did I do?" I'm utterly confused.

"You're so consumed by that book of yours that you're not even listening to what I'm saying."

"Sure I am. You asked what I wanted and I said anything."

"And I gave you multiple choices, one of which I'm *very* eager for you to have."

I purse my lips, trying to recall our conversation, but it doesn't come to mind. When our eyes meet, he takes a step toward me and winks.

I'm screwed.

chapter
FOUR

Parker

I give Aundrea the kind of wink that lets her know I'm not messing around. The kind I know sends shivers all through her.

"Parker." My name comes out sternly and with warning.

I stride slowly toward her. This is an I-want-to-rip-your-clothes-off-right-here-right-now walk. I've had only one thing on my mind since she got frustrated earlier at her computer: having my way with my sexy wife.

"Anything, Aundrea?" Her breath catches at my whisper and her lips part. Her legs fall open, welcoming me, and I don't hide my devious grin.

"Uh-huh."

I lick her full red lips, and I have to hold back the urge to lift her up and devour her right here. She tilts her chin up, trying to make better contact, but I back away swiftly. I do this a couple of times, teasing her. She pouts and groans in frustration when I don't allow her to deepen the kiss. I love tormenting her.

Releasing her mouth, I trace her jaw-line with my tongue. When I reach the spot behind her ear, she shivers. I love that I can cause every single nerve ending in her body to tingle.

"You should be more careful for what you agree to, Aundrea. It could get you into trouble."

"I like getting in trouble with you," she whispers back, closing her eyes at my touch.

I move abruptly, pulling her up from the couch. Her Kindle drops from her lap to the floor with a thud as her chest slams against mine. Our lips meet again, connecting us as one. I can't hold back any longer. I need this woman like she's my last breath. Her hands slip into my shirt, pushing it over my head. I'm greedy, hungry for her, running my hands all over her.

Breaking our kiss, I help Aundrea tug my shirt off, and toss it to the floor. When she reaches for my belt buckle, my hands land over hers, stopping her, and I push her against the wall, causing a hanging art canvas to fall next to us.

A soft cry of pleasure falls from her full lips at the impact and I catch it in my mouth. Our tongues connect and I cup her breasts through her tight T-shirt. Her nipples harden under my fingertips and desire swims through my veins. I can feel my blood coursing through my body, pumping loudly in my ears over our irregular breathing.

I want more from her.

I *need* more from her.

Breaking away, I pull off her shirt, leaving her in a pink lace bra and washed out jeans. I groan with approval and immediately put my mouth to her neck, hooking a finger in her belt loop to tug her closer. I dip my head further down, kissing every inch I can: her neck, shoulders, and cleavage.

"I'm going to take you right here," I groan, pressing my hips into her.

"Yes," she moans, letting her head fall back.

I kiss down her torso and along her abdomen, dropping to my knees. She runs her fingers through my hair, tugging me gently back up her body, but I resist.

I look up at her, resting my chin at the waist of her pants. When she looks down, her hair falls over her shoulders. *God, she's beautiful.* Her eyes plead with me. Slowly, I unzip her pants, never taking my eyes off hers. When she closes them briefly and re-opens them, there is nothing but craving there. Her craving for me.

I tug her pants down and help her step out of them. Once her back is resting against the wall, I pull her thong down to her ankles, not bothering to take them all the way off.

The sound of her head lolling against the wall and the way she parts her legs lets me know she's ready for what's to come. Ever so slowly, I lick my way up her silky smooth skin. She tugs at my hair as I continue the soft strokes of my tongue along her wetness.

"Yes," she breathes out.

Slipping inside of her briefly, then back up to where she's swollen and aching to be touched, I move my tongue faster. Her breathing picks up, as does the tightening of her fingers in my hair. When her hips begin to rock against my face I can't help but smile. I love her taking control, not holding back from getting what she wants.

Reaching behind her, I grasp both her legs at the knees to help brace myself. I continue to work in faster strokes, matching the rhythm of her rocking motion.

"That's it, baby," I manage between breaths.

"I'm … This … Oh, my … Don't …"

I don't stop. I continue until she is spasming against my tongue, taking in every bit that I can.

I trail soft kisses upward toward her mouth.

We lean against the wall for a while, kissing, letting our hands and mouths explore. Something I can do with my eyes closed.

"I want you so bad," she stammers.

Aundrea unzips my pants and slips her hand inside, coming in contact with the soft cotton of my boxers. Just as her fingers brush against my arousal there's a loud knock on our door.

"Ignore it," I huff between kisses. We're not expecting anyone that I can think of.

"I am," she says breathlessly, pushing my jeans down.

The banging picks back up.

"Don't answer that," I say again, with more irritation.

"I won't."

The knocks stop and I smile between our kisses, thrusting into her hand. The pounding starts again, louder this time. "Don't go," she sighs with exasperation when I bend down to pull my pants back up.

I step around Aundrea and head to the door and Aundrea goes into the bedroom so she's not seen standing in her underwear.

"What?" I snap, flinging the door open.

"Surprise!" Genna's smile disappears and her voice goes flat when she sees my unwelcoming face. "Oh, is someone crabby?"

My head drops to my chest. She never calls before coming over.

"Is everything okay?" I'm beyond aggravated.

"Yeah, everything's fine. Jason went in on a call and I was in the area with Hannah," she holds up the baby carrier, "and thought I'd stop in. I talked to Dre earlier and she said you two didn't have plans tonight. Is she here?" she asks hesitantly as her eyes dart over my shoulder.

Well, we *did* have plans. Or rather plans that were in process. Just as I'm about to tell her no, so I can get back to those plans, a quiet voice comes from behind me.

"Yes."

I turn to see Aundrea fully dressed and let out an inner groan of dissatisfaction. Opening the door, I back away, allowing Genna to enter.

"What were you doing?" Genna asks as she steps around me.

Aundrea raises her eyebrows.

"Ohmigod, were you having sex?" she squeals. Yes, Aundrea's thirty-one-year-old sister just squealed in my ear.

"No!" Aundrea exclaims, shocked by her sister's bold words. Her cheeks flush a light shade of rose. God, I love that color on her.

Passing Aundrea, I trace the color with the back of my hand and she leans into me. "I'm sorry," she whispers.

"Don't worry about it." I press a lingering kiss to the top of her head before leaving her alone with Genna.

From the bedroom, I hear part of their conversation.

"What do you need, Genna? Where's Jason?" Aundrea's voice comes out clipped and I must admit I love her feistiness. I make a mental note to bring it out again later.

"He was on call tonight and went in to the clinic. I didn't need anything—sorry. Like I told Parker, I was in the area and thought I'd pop in."

"No, I'm sorry. It's fine. I didn't mean for that to come out the way it did. Come in and sit. We weren't doing anything."

I wouldn't exactly say that.

"I know I have bad timing sometimes, but I figured it's Friday night so you two would be up."

"Yeah, your timing has never been the best." Aundrea giggles and I smile.

"I'm making a mental note to always call before I come over."

Please.

I quickly rinse out my mouth in the bathroom then stretch out in our bed, trying to relax from the interruption of our heated encounter. The soft pillow hugs me and I let my thoughts drift away from their conversation.

The memory of the morning after Aundrea and I met pops into my head. I haven't thought about that morning in a long time. A slow smile forms at the thought of waking up to a loud bang and footsteps leaving my apartment—or, rather, trying to sneak away. I don't think I've ever moved so fast in my life. I almost killed myself getting my feet in my boxers and crashing into the side of the bed. If it hadn't been for my quick reflexes, I would have fallen.

Finding my apartment empty, with no luck in the hallway, I remember slamming my apartment door so hard I thought I knocked it loose from the hinges.

I laugh at the recollection. Breaking my door would have

made me even more pissed.

A weak cry comes from the other room, and gets louder, bringing me out of the pleasant memory. Genna's soothing voice follows.

Getting out of bed, I realize I left my shirt in the living room, so I take a white undershirt off the top of the tall folded pile of laundry. The same pile Aundrea promised she'd put away last week. *Not holding my breath for that to happen.*

I walk into the living room to find Genna sprawled out on our couch. Her feet are crossed at the ankle and her hands are resting behind her head. Aundrea's walking in small circles singing a made-up lullaby to Hannah, who's wrapped securely in a blanket.

In a few short strides, I close the distance to Aundrea and wrap my arm around her waist. I look down at the cute little peanut all snuggled up. She's blowing bubbles and cooing at the buzzing sound her lips make.

"She seems content now."

"Auntie Dre has her," Genna says, giggling.

Aundrea always said she wanted to spoil her sister's kids, and believe me when I say she's spoiling Hannah. She watches her every chance she can get, holding her until her arms can't take it any longer, and buying her anything that—according to her—is "cute and girly."

She's a great aunt. A natural, really. She has a way of knowing what Hannah needs before she cries for it, a way of calming her, and an overall aura that glows around her whenever Hannah's in her arms. This is why I know she'll make a wonderful mom.

I give Aundrea a quick peck on her temple.

"Either of you ladies want a sandwich? I'm going to make one."

"No, thanks," they reply together. Sometimes it's scary how much they sound alike, given how different they are.

Once I've piled meat and cheese on my sandwich to perfection, I rest my shoulder against the doorframe and watch my wife.

Aundrea continues to smile and sing to Hannah. I am transfixed by her. Even in a plain T-shirt and jeans, hair piled in a messy bun on top of her head, and no make-up, she's the most beautiful woman I have ever seen. I take in every curve of her body, the outline of her mouth, the freckles that are perfectly placed on her cheeks, and every strand of her thick beautiful hair that falls around her face. She's just as beautiful as the day I made her my wife, if not more.

When she looks up, our eyes meet. Her smile widens, flashing her white teeth. Her eyes dance with mine and everything around me stops as I zoom in only on her, in what feels like slow motion. Just that one look has me aching. Her smile means everything to me.

Handing Hannah back to Genna she comes over to me, snuggling into my side. Resting her head on my shoulder, she wraps her arms tightly around me.

"You're staring off into space."

"I was?"

She nods. "With a big grin on your face, too. What's on your mind?"

"You," I say, glancing down at her clasped hands that are resting on my side. Her wedding and engagement rings glint up at me. We engraved part of our vows on the inside of each of our wedding bands. It makes me smile every time I look at either of them: a constant reminder of what we mean to one another. Hers says *infinity* and mine says *my love, my life, my friend*. We didn't share the engravings until our wedding day.

"Truth," she teases. "What are you thinking about?"

"That is the truth. I saw your rings and it made me think about our wedding day and, of course, your beautiful smile."

"Is that so?"

I feel her smile into my shoulder. "Yes."

"That was a good day."

"The best."

"You know what will be even better?"

"Hmm?" I don't know what could top that day.

She lowers her voice so only I can hear. "The day we bring home our baby."

"I can't wait for that day, Aundrea."

"Hey, um, I hate to break up this love fest you two have going on, but, Dre, you've yet to give me an answer about next Saturday."

"Hmm?" She breaks away from me, turning to face Genna.

Saturday. I ponder the word, thinking about what next Saturday is, but nothing comes to mind. I see Aundrea trying to recall the same thing, and see the realization cross her face the moment she remembers.

"I already gave you my answer. No, Genna, I am not volunteering at your school's prom. No. Way."

Genna stopped substitute teaching two years ago when she was hired as a full-time English teacher.

"Please, Dre. I'm begging you," Genna pleads. "Don't make me get on my hands and knees."

"No."

"Please?"

"I'm not doing it."

I shake my head at them and take another bite of my sandwich.

"Come on. Think of how much fun we'd have."

"I don't want to go to your prom, Genna. I'm sorry."

Genna lets out a long, heavy sigh. "Fine. But will you at least go dress shopping with me, then? Jean said if I go to the cities she'll be able to hook me up. There's some big trunk show tomorrow."

Trunk show? What the hell is a trunk show?

"I don't know …" Aundrea bites her lip.

"Dreeee," Genna whines like a two-year-old.

"Whaaaat?" Aundrea mocks in the same annoying tone.

Genna laughs. "Please."

"Okay, okay. I want to see Jean anyways."

"Oh thanks."

Aundrea giggles. "What time in the morning?"

"Nine okay?"

"Yes."

"Maybe text Amy and see if she wants to come with? We could make it a girls' day?"

Girls' day. I know what that means. It's when women gather around with drinks and talk about their husbands or boyfriends, then come home and say they didn't.

"That's a great idea! I'm sure she'll love that."

Once Genna leaves I ask Aundrea, "What's this about going to prom?"

Aundrea explains that the school is short on volunteers to chaperone and Genna has been trying to get her to help. "That sounds like fun. I'd even go with you. You know, as your date."

"*That* is exactly why I didn't mention this to you."

"What?" I give her a sinful grin.

"I knew you'd be all for it."

"And that's a problem why?"

She ignores me, walking into our bedroom. I follow quickly on her heels, stripping my shirt off as I go. When she turns around, she shakes her head, smiling.

"What are you doing?"

I wiggle my eyebrows and she swallows. Thoughts of finishing what we started earlier have taken over.

Slowly I pull off my remaining clothes.

"Parker."

I take a few painfully slow steps toward her. "Aundrea." Reaching her, I wrap my arms around her tiny waist, yanking her against me. "Go." Kiss. "To." Kiss. "Prom." Kiss. "With." Kiss. "Me." Kiss.

She exhales, breathlessly. "It's not *our* prom, Parker."

"Who says it can't be? You can't be a college graduate next month without ever having experienced prom."

"Says who?"

"Me. I won't allow it. Now, will you please be my prom date?"

"I have to admit the gesture is sweet."

I push my naked body against hers. "What do you say? I'll pick you up you at six thirty and have you home by eleven," I tease.

She throws her head back, letting out a light laugh. "Are you trying to persuade me with your nakedness?"

"Is it working?"

"As tempting and delicious as that sounds, I'm going to respectfully decline your offer." Her eyes soften. "But I'd be happy to finish what we started in the living room."

I scoop her up, throwing her light frame over my shoulder. Sex now, prom planning later.

"Parker!"

"You asked for it!"

Opening the shower door, I step inside. I have to shift her weight to turn on the shower, and she screams in shock at the sudden coldness as I accidentally put her in the way of the water.

Carefully, I release her and soon enough the water becomes warm. Her clothes are drenched, molding to her curves, and I nod in approval.

"I said the living room. To finish what we started in the *living room.*"

"But this is more fun."

She rolls her eyes as I press my lips to the corner of her mouth.

"I can't believe you're mine," I murmur.

"Only yours."

"Always."

"Always," she repeats.

Aundrea once told me she doesn't believe in only one life. That she believes in souls reconnecting long after death, spending an eternity side by side among the stars.

Aundrea is my life. My eternity.

She's my forever and always.

chapter
FIVE

Aundrea

"**C**ome out. I want to see!" Jean exclaims.

"Yes, come on," Genna adds sweetly.

I can't believe I let them talk me into this. One minute I'm helping Genna decide on a dress, and the next I'm being coerced into trying on a dress myself. Which turned into two dresses, three dresses ... *seven dresses*.

It's not that I didn't think it would be fun, I just wasn't expecting to play dress-up.

Pulling the curtain aside, I step out to face them.

"Dre." Genna grins, water filling her eyes.

"You look ..." Jean's voice falls off as she searches for the right word.

"Stunning," Amy finishes for her.

"Really?" I ask, shocked. That's not the reaction I got to the other dresses.

I turn back to face the mirror and study myself. The autumn orange dress fits like a glove, hugging my body perfectly. There's a long slit up the right side, and gold beads along the bodice coming to rest just above the slit. It really is flattering on me.

I can't help but smile as I take in my appearance. I could

totally see myself wearing this somewhere. Bouncing on my tiptoes with excitement, I turn back to face them.

"It really is a pretty dress."

"Is that a smile I see slipping through," Genna taunts, stepping closer. She reaches out, poking my growing smile.

"Yes," I tease back.

"Okay, hold still. I need to take a picture," Genna announces, handing Hannah to Jean. With her cell phone, she snaps a picture of me posing with one hand on my hip and the other bent at the elbow, resting behind my head. "Great! Mom will love that one!"

I giggle, relaxing my cheesy pose.

We've snapped pictures of each other trying on dresses, texting them to Shannon and my mom as if we're putting on our own runway show. The mini photo shoot reminds me of sitting in the hospital with my mom, receiving texts from my friends as they went dress shopping for our senior prom. It feels good being able to make new memories.

"A dress should never wear you. *You* should wear the dress," Jean proudly explains, handing Hannah back to Genna. "And you, Dre, are wearing this dress. You should get it."

I look down, taking the fabric between my fingers. "I wouldn't have anywhere to wear it." I shrug before turning around and stepping back into the fitting room to change.

"You could wear it this Saturday if you'd agree to volunteer with Jason and me!" Genna's voice carries through the door.

"You talked Jason into going?"

She doesn't answer me. "It will be fun, Dre."

I smile at my reflection in the mirror again, taking in the dress. It's really stunning. A part of me wants to go, but the other part is sure I'll just feel out of place the entire time.

Genna doesn't press the subject.

When we go to pay, the cashier declines Genna's money for her gown, announcing it was already taken care of. Apparently Jean worked it out to have the dress donated, which was extremely nice of her. Since graduating from the University of Minnesota with a major in fashion, she's built professional relationships with some of the top designers in North America. I don't know all the specifics of her job, but I do know she loves it, always looks fantastic, and gets to travel the world.

"Do you three have time for lunch?" Jean asks, glancing at her watch.

I don't need to look. I always have time for my best friend.

We head to a small bistro in the heart of downtown Minneapolis—one of Jean's favorite places to eat.

"This is so good," Genna moans around a bite of whipped chocolate mousse. "I'm so going to try and make this. Oh, that reminds me, are the three of you free in a couple weeks? It doesn't matter when, really, but I'd like to have you over as taste testers. I got hired for my first official Genna's Touch Catering job for a grand opening here in town, and they've asked me to create a full menu for about three hundred people."

When Genna was pregnant she decided to do some catering jobs on the side to help save money for her maternity leave. She didn't expect that she'd have so much fun or that her food would become such a huge hit. When she started getting calls from small businesses wanting to hire her, she decided that she's going to resign from her teaching position at the end of the year and turn her passion for cooking into a business. Jason is fully on board and they've decided to remodel their kitchen, transforming it into a chef's dream.

Jean whistles. "Damn."

"Wow," Amy stammers. "Nothing like getting started out."

"Good for you! And, of course, count me in," I say excitedly.

"Me too."

"Of course I'll be there!"

"Great!" She grins. "If Kevin, Parker, and Brandon are up for it they can come too. It could be fun. Oh, Amy, Ethan is more than welcome to come, too."

"Thanks, Genna. I'm sure he'd like that."

"That sounds like a great idea," I say.

Jean scoffs and I raise my eyebrows. She doesn't answer right away, just sighs. "That just sounds too much like a couple thing."

"Couple thing?" Genna and I ask together, looking at one another.

She shrugs. "Yeah, you know, where you arrive together, sit together and smile, and then go home together."

"Wait, I'm confused. Umm? Aren't you and Kevin together? For like almost two years now," I remind her. She ignores me, taking a bite of fruit salad.

At first, Kevin was the last person I wanted to see my best friend date because he can be immature at times but, overall, he's a decent guy and makes her happy.

"Eh, technicalities. We're more like two adults who happen to enjoy sex with each other and don't mind hanging out afterward."

According to her, it was "fuck at first sight." They met at our engagement party, slept together that night—or, the next day, if we're getting technical—and haven't been able to stop since. They're a couple.

"Whatever you say." I give her a teasing smile, but her eyes flash at me warningly.

"And when do you move into the house?" she inquires.

"What house? You bought a house? How come I didn't know this?" Genna practically chokes as she coughs down the bite of bread she had in her mouth.

Amy cocks her head, surprised that my sister doesn't know.

Jean's eyes dance between Genna and me laughingly.

"What's so funny?" I ask.

"Nothing." She chuckles. "I just find it a little funny you

didn't tell your own sister about your anniversary present."

"Same here." Amy giggles, then covers her mouth, trying to force herself to stop, but can't.

Genna's scowl darkens. Her naturally pale skin begins to form a light crimson color. "Wait! *That* was your anniversary present. You said you went for a drive."

I roll my eyes. "I was starting to tell you the story, but Hannah got fussy and you had to go. You never called me back and I haven't talked to you since."

"Um, last night," she says emphatically, she stays completely relaxed as she rocks a sleeping Hannah in her arms.

I think about last night and what she interrupted. "I wasn't really in the mood to discuss anything last night."

"Because you were having sex before I arrived."

I blush a little. Talking about my sex life never gets easier. Sometimes I wish I was more open, like Jean.

Jean perks up. "This is getting good." *Or maybe not.*

Ignoring them, I keep my focus on Genna. "I meant to tell you. I'm telling you now. I'm sorry." I give her my best little sister smile, which is more of a pout with pleading, soft eyes, which always makes her laugh.

She tries to fight her smile, but her mouth eventually gives way. "You're forgiven. Now, tell me all about this beautiful house. I want to know where it is, how many rooms, the colors, layout, kitchen, everything."

I shake my head. She's exactly like my mom. Way too detail-oriented.

Amy starts to describe the house before I can, not hiding her excitement. Eventually she lets me join in, telling Genna every detail, down to the crown molding.

Hannah slowly wakes up, smacking her lips and opening and closing her mouth.

"Is somebody hungry? I ask in my best baby voice.

"She sure is."

When Genna pulls out a bottle I offer to feed Hannah, reaching across the table to take her.

"Soon that will be you, Dre." I hear the love in Genna's voice, but I tense. *How does she know?*

Amy's mouth opens but I shake my head at her and she nods.

"Well, um, actually …" Genna and Jean look at me with anticipation while Amy grins. "Parker and I have decided that we're going to start looking into agencies to help us find a surrogate."

"A baby!" Jean squeaks.

Genna breaks out into a huge smile and her eyes go all soft. "Dre, you're having a baby?"

"Not right now," I tease. "It's going to be a process, but one we're ready to start."

"Dre," Genna whispers, "I'm so happy for you." She stands and gives me a gentle hug, careful not to disrupt Hannah.

"Have you told Mom yet?" she asks, smiling wide.

I shake my head. "No, but soon. I want something solid to tell her before I get her excited."

I glance at Jean, making sure she's okay after her loud screech of "A baby!" Her head is shaking, mouth ajar, face stunned, and her newly cut bob is swirling around her face with each head bobble.

"Jean?" I say cautiously.

"I'm at a loss for words, but I'm happy for you. You know that, right? I'll always be in your corner, supporting you, Dre."

"I know."

Jean knows every fear of mine. She has since we were kids. I know she's probably stunned at our decision to have a child, but I also know she's happy for me and that she'll have my back. No matter what.

"I couldn't be happier for her. When she told me, I had the same reaction." Amy gives me a warm smile.

"You knew?" Genna asks, stunned.

"Yes."

Genna looks my way, shocked, and I give a sympathetic

shrug. Genna just doesn't like feeling left out.

"I saw her at Mayo and she told me all about it." Amy recovers quickly.

"Did you find an agency?" Genna asks.

I nod. "An independent company just outside of Rochester called Circle of Life. I fell in love with their mission and I think Parker was just happy to be done searching." Or maybe it was the other way around. I smile, remembering last night. "I'm going to call on Monday to schedule an appointment. I promise you'll be the first to know when we sign, Genna."

She gives me a pleased smile.

The discussion quickly turns to baby names, Genna's suggestions making us all laugh. I'm not sure how she comes up with some of them so fast, considering I'm not sure a lot of them are even real names.

I like thinking that someday Parker and I will be having this discussion and I doubt it will be an easy decision.

Even though I didn't see this part of my life at one time, I see it now. This is how everything was supposed to turn out. Being a wife, having a great career, a family, and the support of those that mean the most to me.

~⊙ ⊙~

I called The Circle of Life first thing Monday and scheduled an appointment with them for today, since my last final exam was yesterday.

The drive to the agency is about forty-five minutes. We don't speak, but hold hands tightly the entire drive.

When we walk into the waiting room, tension is thick, stress and apprehension written all over the faces of the hopeful parents. It's almost painful to see. I'd imagined walking into a room filled with bright colors and smiling faces, not dim lighting and worried expressions.

Parker gives my hand a quick reassuring squeeze as we approach the desk.

"Good morning; how can I help you?" the receptionist

asks with a smile.

"Good morning. We have a ten o'clock appointment with Polly," Parker answers.

She looks down at her computer screen, does some button pushing, and then grabs a stack of paperwork, handing it to Parker on a clipboard with a pen. "If you could please fill these out and bring them back once they're completed, I'll let her know you'll be ready as soon as you're done."

We flip through each page, answering questions about our income, desired surrogate location, and medical history, reminding me of why we're here in the first place.

"Desired location?" I whisper to Parker. "Who wouldn't want someone from the same area carrying their baby?"

He shrugs. "I don't know. Maybe it helps if you're not picky about the location?"

"Huh."

We didn't really discuss looking outside the Twin Cities. Quite honestly, I didn't even consider it an option. I want to be near the woman who's going to be carrying our child.

After the paperwork is filled out, we sit in silence, flipping through magazines until our names are called.

We're taken to a quiet office by a tall blonde who asks us to be seated. "Polly will be with you in a couple of minutes. Would either of you like something to drink? Coffee or water?"

"No, thank you."

"I'm good, thanks."

I'm too nervous to drink anything, afraid if I do I may end up peeing my pants. I'm anxious, yet excited.

Soon we're greeted by a quiet knock. "Good morning," a sweet voice says. I turn in my chair to get the first glimpse at the woman who will help decide our fate. She's older, with short, curly brown hair and cute small-framed glasses.

"Hello," we reply.

Parker stands to greet her, towering over her. I stay seated, waiting for them to finish their greeting.

"I'm Polly. It's so nice to meet the two of you."

"Likewise," Parker says.

Taking her seat, Polly asks, "Why don't you tell me about yourselves and what you're interested in."

She listens carefully, making notes as we take turns speaking.

"At this point, we're really interested in knowing what to expect in terms of cost, time-line, et cetera," Parker concludes.

"Of course. First, I've looked over Aundrea's history and," she pauses, looking at me, "it looks like you underwent a transvaginal oocyte retrieval about seven years ago before starting chemotherapy for Hodgkin's Lymphoma, correct?"

I bite the inside of my cheek. I knew I'd have to discuss my history—and, hence, why we're here—but it doesn't make it easier talking about it with a complete stranger. "That's correct."

"And they're stored where, exactly?"

"At Twin Cities Fertility Specialists. Do you work with them?" I ask as she writes the name down. I'm not sure what the process of transporting the eggs entails, or what the cost of something like that would even be.

"We have, yes, and we'd have your surrogate go there for the implantation process, which is something you would list in your contract with her, as well as pay the transportation fees for. But we'll get to all that in a minute." She glances at the papers in her hand before turning back to me. "The embryos have not been created, correct?"

"Right."

"I would recommend getting that started. It's an easy process and can be done with Twin Cities Fertility. You won't need us for that, and it will help with the process once a surrogate is selected for the two of you."

"What exactly is that process?" Parker asks, glancing my way.

"Honestly, not much, aside from the drive and your donation, Parker. Basically, you'll schedule an appointment and drop off a specimen, which the clinic will transfer into the egg. The embryo will take about three to five days to develop. Those will be frozen until they're needed for the transfer. As far as how many embryos you choose to create is entirely up to you, but the specialist with the clinic may suggest a number."

"That sounds easy enough," Parker says.

The knots in my stomach are replaced with butterflies at the thought of creating a child with Parker. It may not be the typical way, but it's *our* way.

"Here is our packet." She hands us a folder containing a thick stack of papers and three brochures: Coping with Your Surrogate, Is Surrogacy Right for You, and Finding the Perfect Match. We scoot our chairs closer together to look it over.

"You're looking at about a year and half to two years until you have a baby in your arms. However, you need to understand that this is just a general time frame we give all our clients."

We both nod, flipping through the papers.

I can handle that time frame.

"We will look in our system for a carrier match in the location you requested and set up the meeting for you. If you feel it's a good match, then the legal contracts will be drawn. As the intended parents, you will cover all legal fees for you and the carrier. She is entitled to use her own lawyer, however, we do offer one to represent all surrogates in our agency if she so chooses."

"Sure, that won't be a problem," Parker says calmly.

I look over at him. *Not a problem?* We were just approved for a house loan. Does he think we're growing a money tree?

"Do we need to find our own lawyer, or do you have one that represents the parents too?" I ask.

"Yes, we do work closely with a firm but, again, you're free to use your own lawyer if you choose. Shall we go through the information?"

Polly goes over the costs, what to expect, and the process, including the exact timeline of the procedure. Parker takes in everything, asking questions and replying to them. I try to write down as much as I can, but mostly I find myself staring at the packet before me, dollar signs flashing off the pages. What it comes down to is that having a baby will cost us somewhere between sixty and eighty thousand dollars. As the intended parents, we're responsible to cover all agency costs, surrogate fees, medical costs, and insurance coverage, maternity leave, clothing allowance, transportation when necessary, legal and psychiatric evaluation fees.

"There are two types of surrogacy listed. Which one would we be doing?" I ask, pointing at the paper in my hand.

"You'll go through a Gestational Surrogacy because you already have your eggs and the embryos will be created and implanted into your surrogate. This process can be a little faster, too. There are some hormones your surrogate will need to take to prepare for the implantation but, besides that, you're looking at saving yourself a few extra months, as well as dollars. Another big savings, of course, is if you have your own surrogate. Have you discussed this? Some use a family member or close friend." We look at each other. I never even thought about that. "It's a savings of about twenty-five thousand dollars."

"No, I don't think we even thought about asking someone we knew," Parker says.

Who would we even ask?

"It might be something to discuss. Our requirements are in the back of your packet. The major ones being that she has given birth to a healthy child in the last ten years and is under the age of thirty-two at the time of implantation."

That leaves out Jean and Shannon.

"How long between pregnancies?" I'm not sure I'd ask Genna, but it might be worth discussing.

"Three months from a vaginal delivery and six months from a C-section. Do you have someone in mind?"

"My sister, but I'm not even sure she'd be up to it. She had a baby a couple months ago, and …" I trail off, unsure what else to add. Parker and I have a lot to discuss and think about.

"If she's interested, we'd love to meet with her. She'd have to go through psychiatric and physical evaluations first, but it would definitely help your process move along faster."

"We'll have to talk about it."

"You two don't need to make any decisions today. It's a lot to take in, so go home, think about it, and call me with any questions. If your sister has any questions she can certainly call too. I know this can all be overwhelming."

"If we choose not to use a family member, how long are you thinking until we have a surrogate match?" I ask.

"That can be tricky. With your selective area I would anticipate at least four to six months. We have a few in our system in the Minneapolis area but, as of now, they're already matched. But we do have new clients coming in all the time. It's rare a match falls through, but it does happen."

"Okay." Six months. I can handle that. I mentally make a timeline. We'd have to have contracts drawn up and agreed upon, which could take a while, we'd need a month or two for hormones before the implantation, then at least two weeks until we find out if we're pregnant, and, if all goes well, a baby nine months later. We're looking at just under two years. That sounds very reasonable.

I take a deep breath and let it out slowly. This is good. I feel good about all this.

"That all sounds great," Parker says, and we smile at one another. I take his hand, giving the back of it a quick peck.

"Good! I'm glad to hear that. So, if you two decide to sign with us, the signing fee we discussed is in the paperwork. We require half at the time of signing, twenty-five percent when the contract with the surrogate is signed, and the last part within seven days of delivery. All other fees associated with the surrogate will be drawn up in the contract."

I'm excited, but I also can't help the nerves I feel. I didn't except this to cost so much. But, then again, can you really put a price on a baby?

We say our goodbyes and Polly walks us out to the waiting area. Parker leads the way to the elevator and to our car.

Once we're in a space where we feel we can talk freely, we both start at once.

"I want this."

"Let's sign!"

"Really?" he asks me, turning in his seat with a shy grin.

"Of course!"

"So, we're really going to have a baby?"

I don't know why he needs the reassurance, but I give it to him. "We're really going to have a baby."

He leans over the center console, his mouth landing on mine.

After our lips break apart, he leans back.

"Do you think you'd be interested in asking Genna to be our surrogate?"

My lips purse. "I'm not sure how I'd feel about watching my sister carry our child."

"What do you mean?"

"Well, for starters, all during her pregnancy with Hannah, she talked about forming that special bond with her unborn child. I don't think I'd be able to handle watching that bond form between her and our baby." He nods. "I can only imagine it would make bringing the baby home all the more difficult, too. I think I'd feel like I was stealing her baby, and not bringing home *our* baby. Using a stranger would be easier, I think. There's no emotional connection between us and her."

"I understand where you're coming from. If it makes you feel more comfortable, I have absolutely no problem looking into using one of the agency's surrogates."

"I think Genna would be great." I need him to know that. It's not that I don't want to ask her.

"I know you do."

"I just want this to be about us, with no pressure from family involved. And, God forbid if anything were to happen, I wouldn't want her to feel responsible."

"I think you're right. In the end, it's best we use someone

with no connection to us."

"Yes."

Once we're on the road, Parker takes my hand and our fingers lock together. I squeeze tight, needing him to not let go of me. Or maybe it's me not wanting to let go of him and this moment. Because, right now, holding his hand and thinking about the decisions we have made and will continue to make, I believe that no matter what happens, we're in this.

Together.

chapter

SIX

Aundrea

On Saturday, I spend the afternoon helping Genna get ready for what she calls "prom day." I'm not the best at doing hair and make-up, but I've learned a few tricks over the last couple of years, thanks to Jean. When it's time for her to leave, I drive back to the apartment.

I enter the apartment, calling for Parker. Silence. I yell again, even though the place isn't that big.

When I walk into the bedroom my eyes widen. Lying in the center of the bed is the orange dress that I tried on at the dress shop. Next to it is a note that says, "Wear me."

I pick the dress up, stunned. "What the?"

"Do you like it?" a raspy voice startles me.

Whipping around, my mouth drops open. Parker's standing behind me with his hands behind his back, dressed in a black tux and an orange vest that matches the dress I'm holding.

I step in front of him, running my fingers across the soft stubble along his chin. I love his stubble. He wanted to shave it when we got married, but I told him he was never allowed to shave his face clean. Ever.

"What's going on?" I whisper.

"I know you didn't want to be a chaperone at the prom tonight, but you deserve to experience a prom, Aundrea, even if it's just volunteering." Parker fumbles with clear plastic packaging.

"Parker Cade Jackson, are you blushing?"

He looks up. "I want this to be perfect."

"What?"

"Tonight."

He continues opening the box, slowly, looking nervous as he takes out a flower. It's a white and pink corsage. His takes my right wrist, slipping the elastic band over my now shaking hand.

"Aundrea, will you do me the honor of being my prom date this evening?"

"You got me a corsage?" I whisper, admiring the beautiful colors.

"It's a lotus. Lotus means rebirth. I believe there are stages in our life, no matter our past or our age, which we deserve to be given a second chance at—a rebirth of something we missed out on. This is one of those second chances. An opportunity for you to experience something that you weren't able to the first time."

My eyes burn. How on earth did I get so lucky as to call the man before me my husband? I've spent every day thanking whoever is above for watching over me the day Parker walked into my life.

"I don't know how it can't be perfect with you as my date," I say, leaning into him and wrapping my arms around his waist, pulling us closer together.

"I want tonight to be flawless for you. I want to give you the most perfect damned prom you've ever dreamed of."

Prom. It's just a word to some. But for me, it's a key. A key that unlocks a painful memory and lets it free.

∽♊︎∼

Clipping the last piece of my curled hair back into a low

bun at the nape of my neck, I take in the sleek dress that clings to my body.

"I don't want to rush perfection, but are you ready?" Parker calls from the living room.

"Two more seconds."

I apply a last swipe of lip-gloss, one more coat of mascara, and a little pink glimmer blush. I know this isn't my prom, but tonight *is* my night, so I'm going to look the best I can.

Nodding in approval, I shut off the bedroom light and walk into the living room to greet Parker.

He stands up immediately when I enter. "Wow," he stutters under his breath. "Aundrea, you look … remarkable." He blinks a few times before stepping closer to me. Taking my hand, he gives me a small spin, taking in every inch of me.

When he doesn't speak, I give him a warm smile. I feel my heart pounding against my chest. I don't know why I'm so nervous, but right now I feel as if I really am seventeen again and waiting to go to the prom—but this time it's so much better.

"You don't look half bad yourself, handsome."

"Not half bad? I didn't get my nickname looking not half bad."

I giggle. "No, I suppose you didn't."

He looks so young in this moment. Almost shy. "I'm honestly … wow," he says, as he runs his hand through his blond hair again.

"Oh, come on!" I nudge him. "*You* speechless? I didn't think such a thing was possible."

"I mean it. Aundrea, you look … that dress!"

I feel the blush creeping up my cheeks. I love that this man can still make the butterflies inside flutter. "Thank you." Now I'm the one who's speechless.

Parker holds out his arm and I link mine with his. "Come on, beautiful. Genna instructed that I have us arrive no later than seven. I can't have you late."

In true Parker fashion, we pull into the Convention Center

parking lot in record time. A few heads in the parking lot turn and watch us pull in. I'm sure they're more interested in his Scion FRS than the people inside.

A group of teens are hanging out by the entrance, laughing and smiling as they pose for pictures. The girls look like delicate princesses in their beautiful ball gowns, showing off huge smiles and holding tightly to their dates. Watching them makes me think back to the pictures I received from my friends when I couldn't make it to prom.

Parker opens my door, extending his hand to me.

"Thank you," I say softly. My short-heeled nude shoes clack against the pavement as I step out. I feel a little out of place as I glance at the line of limos dropping off the late arrivals.

"You okay?"

"What, you can read minds now?"

He laughs. "No, you just have that look on your face like you're getting ready to run."

"I am," I say, only half joking.

Parker and I link arms. I see some confused looks out of the corner of my eye as we make our way to the front entrance.

"Do you think they're wondering who these old folks are crashing their prom?" Parker jokes.

"Hey, buddy, the only old person here is you."

Stopping, he turns to face me with a stern look. "Are you calling me old?"

"No, I'd never suggest such a thing." I giggle at his sad expression.

"You didn't think I was too old last night," he retorts.

"Oh, no." I shake my head. "You were definitely not too old last night."

We walk through the front entrance and into the large ballroom. *Wow.* The place has been transformed into a tropical island. Everywhere you look, white twinkle lights set a romantic mood. Lighted palm trees line a handmade walkway that looks like sand and leads to round tables with big red umbrellas that are set up for dinner. There are cabanas along the back of the room, more palm trees bracketing a line of hammocks, and food stations decorated with little tiki carvings for a buffet. On the back wall, large letters spell A Night in Paradise. There have to be at least five hundred people here, students, teachers, and volunteers dancing and mingling.

"Damn, this blows my prom out of the water," Parker declares, looking around with a stunned expression.

Is this what I was missing out on? I ask myself, still gaping at the beautiful room. Ellie Goulding's "Anything Can Happen" is blaring through the speakers. I love this song.

"Hey guys!" Genna calls from behind us. Turning, I see her and Jason walking toward us. Genna looks stunning in her long, purple, beaded halter dress. There's definitely no evidence that she had a baby a few months back.

"Hey, Genna. This place is—"

"Something, huh?" she finishes for me.

"Did the students do this?"

"Those on the prom committee, along with some teachers and parents. They've been working on it all week, but planning for months."

"It's awesome. So, where do you want us? What's on the agenda?"

"You two will be in this room with Jason and me. It's simple, really. We need to make sure the students behave and don't leave the area except to go to the bathroom. If they do leave, they have to go out the main entrance, and there is no re-entry."

"Sounds easy enough," Parker says, wrapping his arm around my waist.

"We have a great group of kids here. I doubt there will be any problems."

As the night progresses, the four of us spend our time near the dance floor, laughing and chatting about the students.

"I can't wait to get you out of this dress," Parker whispers into my ear as he traces a finger down my neck.

I look over my shoulder, meeting his passionate gaze. "I mean it, Aundrea. You look so good. Every time you move, that dress just clings tighter to you and all I can think about is getting you out of it." I love how husky his voice is when he whispers. It's low and seductive, causing my heart to beat like a drum.

"Parker," I say, bashful.

"Oh, come on beautiful, don't tell me you can't wait for me to get inside of you." Heat washes over me. I glance around the room but no one is paying us any attention.

"I can't wait," I whisper back.

He gives me a wink before turning his attention back to the students.

When Josh Groban's "When You Say You Love Me" comes on, Parker drags me onto the dance floor, moving as close as he can get. It's our song. We danced to it at our wedding. We spent the entire night on the dance floor. It didn't matter if the song was slow or fast, we never left, laughing the night away. It was one of the best nights of my life.

"You made my heart stop tonight, Aundrea. I don't think I can tell you enough how beautiful you look," Parker murmurs.

"You make mine stop at least once a day," I reply, looking into his eyes.

"I hope it never stops, beautiful. Ever."

As the song comes to an end, he leans down and whispers seductively, "I got a room tonight."

Tilting my head to get a better look at him, I mouth, "A room?"

His lips brush my ear, whiskers lightly tickling my neck. "A hotel. I promise I'll have you home by curfew … unless you're feeling naughty."

I give him a wicked smirk. "I don't like to follow the rules."

"I didn't think so." He kisses my temple and clasps my hand, leading me to the other side of the ballroom.

He whisks me off the dance floor toward the exit sign,

but veers left instead.

"Where are we going? What about the room?"

"I've been a horrible date and forgot one of the most important things."

"What's that?"

"Our picture."

"I think that's only for the students, Parker."

"Nonsense. It's our prom. Besides, I promised you a night you wouldn't forget. That includes a keepsake picture."

"I thought making it a night we won't forget is what the hotel room was for?"

"Oh, trust me; it will be. But, first things first. Come on."

With our fingers intertwined, he takes me to the photo station. Parker wraps his arms around my waist, and my hands come down on top of his. Being here with him and seeing how much he's trying to give me the prom I never had reminds me of just how lucky I truly am. Not that I've ever questioned it, but it shows how he'll continue to stop at nothing to give me the life I was always meant to have.

I glance down at the lotus on my wrist. He's giving me a rebirth.

chapter SEVEN

Parker

The second the school doors close behind us, I scoop Aundrea up in my arms and carry her to the car. She lets out a shriek of surprise, but quickly relaxes. The light wind blows a few strands of hair across her face and I bend down, kissing the top of her head. The scent of her coconut shampoo is intoxicating.

Genna and Jason come out after us, laughing like two teenagers in love. "Thanks guys! I had so much fun," Genna yells as they walk away.

"It was a lot of fun," I call back. "Thank you."

"Yeah, thank you," Aundrea adds. "Surprisingly, I enjoyed myself." She looks at me. "Thank you for giving me this. I needed it."

"You're welcome." I'd give her the world if I could. Looking over toward Genna and Jason, I quip, "If you'll excuse us, we're going to be off like a prom dress." I can't even get the last word out before I'm laughing at my own immature joke. *Hey, I'm reliving my senior year!*

"Parker!" Aundrea playfully swats my shoulder and Jason laughs from across the parking lot.

"That a guy! Go get 'em!" he says, and whistles. Genna's

faint giggle echoes off the cars.

"Men," Aundrea snorts into my chest, and I grin.

The parking lot is dim and all I hear are passing cars and the distant strains of music from the ballroom.

"Really, thank you for getting me to come tonight," Aundrea says softly.

I think of what's about to happen.

"Oh, you'll be coming, all right."

"You seem so confident." She gives me an I-dare-you look.

That's because I am. "Always, babe. Always."

Her chin presses into my chest. I can sense her smile. I love that smile.

At the car, I set her down and help her in, giving her a smile as I cross to the driver's side. Her hopeful expression makes me determined to make the rest of our night as good as the prom.

I can feel her eyes on me as I drive. She doesn't speak right away, but I know she's contemplating something. A few more seconds go by before I see the tremble in her mouth.

"Did you really get a hotel room?"

I knew she'd like the idea. "Of course. It's prom night after all." I waggle my eyebrows, which gets a sweet, soft laugh. I love feeling like I'm seventeen again. "Why? Are you saying you can't wait that long?" I'm not teasing anymore.

She doesn't answer. It's all the confirmation I need.

I turn the wheel sharply, and her shoulder hits the door. *Oops! Maybe I should have planned that move a little better.*

Her laugh falls flat and her face is blank as I pull over. The few cars behind us speed by.

"Parker, what are you doing?"

I undo my seatbelt and face her, tucking a curl behind her ear. I put a hand on her inner thigh, just where her skin peeks through the slit in her dress.

Her breath catches and I grin. I love that sound. Her skin is so soft and I can tell by her rapid breathing and goosebumps that my touch has sent her into a tailspin.

Her eyes go wide as I move close, our noses nearly touching. I lick my lips. "Do you think you can wait for the hotel?" I whisper. I trace her upper lip with my tongue. "So sweet," I groan.

"Parker …"

My breathing is shallow. "You can't wait, can you?" I mumble the words against her lips.

"No."

I blindly reach to shut the car off. *We're going to be here a while.*

I am getting harder by the second and can only imagine the pressure that's building between her thighs. I can sense how much she wants to kiss me, so I back away playfully. I love teasing her. Tempting her. Her moans make me yearn for her.

"You're so sexy in this dress, Aundrea. Since I first saw you in it, all I wanted was to get you out. And I will. Soon. But first, I'm going to get a small taste." I slide my fingers up her thigh and under her dress.

"Wait, what if we get caught?" Her eyes go wide and shocked.

"Living on the edge, babe."

That's all she needed to hear. Her legs fall open, giving me all the access I need, and I groan.

She closes her eyes tightly when I touch her.

"I'm going to make you feel so good." I shift in my seat, adjusting myself in my suddenly too-tight pants. I need to be inside of her.

Soon.

I lean over her, easing her seat back.

"Just relax," I whisper against her mouth.

She opens her mouth to speak, but closes it right away. She throws her hands around my neck, tugging me closer. I oblige, considering the tight space. This car was not made for making out, much less for sex.

My mouth is on hers and our tongues join, gliding against each other. She sucks on my bottom lip and bites down gently. She knows it drives me crazy.

I pull down the top of her dress, and her head falls back as I taste her.

"Please …"

"No need to beg, babe. I got you."

I ease the thin fabric of her underwear aside and thrust two fingers deep inside of her. She cries out in pleasure and her hips rock as I work my fingers in and out of her, spreading her wetness around.

"You feel amazing. Slippery and wet."

"God, yes."

"God isn't here, honey. It's just you and me."

"Parker."

"That's it. Say it again."

"Parker."

I rub the swollen bud that screams for my touch and she begins to tremble.

"Right there, please!"

I'm practically on top of her and I wiggle to try and find a more comfortable position in this cramped car, but when I realize that isn't happening, I ignore the small cramp in my side and focus on Aundrea.

I can see the lights from cars driving by, but I couldn't care less. It doesn't matter to me that we're in the middle of town on the side of the road. The only thing I care about is making Aundrea scream my name.

Her hips buck against my hand as I ease my fingers back inside of her. Soft and gentle. In and out. I rub my thumb against her, making her cry out, then I move my fingers faster. Her breathing picks up, then she's shaking, erupting, and tightening around me.

"That's it," I groan, feeling her orgasm.

I watch her face. Watch her eyes tighten and her lips part as she comes down from her high. I could watch her like this all day.

"You are so sexy when you come."

Her cheeks turn pink and her chest flushes. She covers

her face, embarrassed.

"Don't hide." I pull her hands away. "You're beautiful, Aundrea, and I love that I'm the only one who gets to experience that face. To know that beautiful expression is there because of me."

She doesn't say anything, but her expression turns devilish. A look that lets me knows she's plotting something sinful.

"We have a room."

Sitting up, she moves with me, pushing against my chest. I climb back into my seat and she puts her seat back up, adjusting her dress as she sits up.

"I know, but what fun is that when we have right here, right now?"

"This was only meant to be a quick stop, considering you couldn't wait."

She raises an eyebrow at me. "I don't think *either* of us could wait."

I groan. She's making this so difficult on me. I have a mental fight with myself while staring into her damned hazy, love-filled eyes. A part of me wants to take her right here, even though I know it won't be comfortable for either of us, while the other part wants to wait until we get to the room. After all, that's where I intended the night to end.

"Parker?"

My decision is made when she pulls her dress all the way up to her waist.

"Hold on!" Reaching out quickly, I stop her. With a hand on either side of her hips, I hold her in place. "As tempting as you are, I have to stop you right there."

She gives me a pout.

"I know, I know." I trace her bottom lip, lingering there with my finger. Her eyes close at my touch. "I'm seriously kicking myself right now because Lord knows I want to take you right now, but I can't. I promised you a night you wouldn't forget, and that includes the big finish."

"I thought that's what we were doing?"

Taking a deep breath, I count to five. When I know I have a grip on the situation I begin to roll her scrunched dress back down her legs, watching her silky smooth skin disappear.

"This was only a preview."

I don't think I can get to the hotel fast enough once we're back on the road. I'm not certain I've come to complete stops when I'm supposed to, and I haven't even considered slowing down at yellow lights. All I can think about is how good she felt beneath my touch, and how I want more.

The hotel isn't that far from the Convention Center. Only a few miles. Or, maybe it only seems that close because of the speed I'm driving.

Finally, we get there. I clasp Aundrea's hand and make a beeline for the stairway. I can't take another moment of torture, and waiting for the elevators sounds like exactly that right now.

"What about checking in?" Aundrea mumbles as I pull her past the front desk, almost stumbling.

"Already taken care."

"When?"

"Earlier." I spent the afternoon here getting it set up while Aundrea was with Genna. It's nothing major, but I figured if we're doing prom then she should get the whole experience, which includes the romantic hotel room at the end of the perfect night.

I only let go of her hand long enough to unlock the door.

"Oh. My. Parker. This is, wow." Her eyes are wide and her voice quiet.

I've placed pink lotus flowers all around the room. Dozens of battery-operated tea lights form a path along the red and blue carpet, cover the dresser, and illuminate the bed, which is covered in pink petals.

"You did all this … for me?"

Of course I did, but she already knows that. I take her hands and pull her inside. I didn't come here to talk and I know she didn't either.

Her lips turn up at the corners as she follows me.

When I hit the corner of the bed I stumble backward. I brace myself, but not quickly enough. Before I even know what's happening, Aundrea pushes me flat on the mattress. I land on a few tea lights and grunt in annoyance, tossing them aside. Well, it seemed like a good idea to put them here at the time.

Aundrea straddles me.

I can't take my eyes off her as she tugs her dress up to her waist. Her hips shift against me and the hard bulge in my pants responds.

"Is this what you wanted?" she whispers, leaning into me. Her cleavage is pronounced, and my eyes linger there for a few moments.

My breathing quickens when she slowly taunts me, leaning back slightly and unzipping her dress. I can't wait another second. I sit up and tug her zipper down forcefully. She lets out a tiny yelp of surprise.

"You're all I want."

I kiss her neck and her chest, pushing her bra down and cupping her swollen breasts in my hands. Her head falls back, and before long she's pushing back on her heels. I look up at her, waiting.

"I think it's only fair I make you feel good, don't you think?" she says, giving me a grin that makes me want to lose myself right here.

Fuck. "Aundrea." I don't smile. "Are you insinuating what I think you are?"

"I don't know, but if you're talking about me riding you, you would be correct."

Good God! "Jesus, woman."

"Jesus isn't here." Her face stays serious as she uses my cheesy line and I try hard not to laugh. I can tell she's trying just as hard, but a small snicker escapes anyway.

I grin at her, but when she stands and slips out of her clothing all memories of our joke are gone.

"You have such an amazing body, Aundrea. So sexy," I murmur, leaning back on my elbows as I watch her.

As she climbs on top of me, I lie back. She begins slowly grinding her hips into mine, and I get even harder.

Our lips join and she pulls my zipper down. I suck on her top lip as she rubs me, but my head falls back when her hand slips inside my boxers, taking my hard length into her palm.

She lightly traces up and down my shaft, setting it free from my clothing. My breathing speeds up with her movements.

All I can think about is being inside of her and feeling her soft body around me.

I cup her cheek and hold her head, deepening our kiss. It feels as if flames are leaping between Aundrea's skin and mine, igniting us.

She shifts her hips, positioning herself and I am desperate. If this woman doesn't let me bury myself deep inside of her soon, I'll embarrass myself. She giggles, clearly aware of my desperation, and glides down slowly, taking in every inch of me. I thrust up, needing to be deeper inside her.

"Shit," I mutter. She is so warm and tight and I'm already close, so I hold her hips in place, trying to settle down a little. I want us to take our time. I need to enjoy every minute of this.

Aundrea lifts up so I'm almost all the way out of her, then slams back down on me, pulling swears from me over and over.

She finds a rhythm she likes, rocking against me. I keep my hands on her hips, but let her set the pace.

"Fuck, Aundrea. You're so fucking hot right now."

She opens her eyes and I can see the fire burning behind them; I'm sure she can see the desire in mine.

I react without a thought: still inside her, I reverse our positions, putting her beneath me.

"Parker!" she gasps in surprise.

I pull out and thrust back inside of her. She arches and her eyes roll back.

"Oh my ..."

"That's it, baby."

I pull out and push myself back in, slowly. I suddenly realize that I'm still clothed while she's naked. Somehow, that makes it even hotter.

Our bodies move as one, seeking pleasure.

My shirt is clinging to me, drenched in sweat with the exertion of my powerful thrusts. I am blazing hot as Aundrea moves her hips faster and I push as deep as I can.

"Parker, oh my God, don't stop. Right there," she calls out. *God, yes.* I love giving this woman pleasure.

"No fucking way am I stopping."

I squeeze her breasts, rolling her nipples between my fingertips.

"Yes," she moans.

I'm an inferno, the fire inside me raging as I shudder, erupting with my pleasure, and emptying my release inside of her.

Hers isn't far behind. She tightens around me and I kiss her damp hair as she lets out the breath she was holding.

"Holy shit, Aundrea." There's no other sound but our heaving breaths and the clicking of what sounds like the air conditioning wanting to come on. "You are one hell of a woman."

"I could say the same about you."

I raise an eyebrow.

"I mean," she pauses, laughing, "you're one hell of a man." She laughs harder.

"You bet your sweet ass I'm a man. All man," I say moving my hips so she can feel just how much of a man I am, still inside her.

Her eyes dance and she grins up at me. "Definitely all man."

I ease out of her and drop a kiss on her collarbone, allowing her to slide farther up the bed. The petals are everywhere and the comforter is disheveled from our movements.

I quickly undress, needing to get out of these hot, sticky clothes.

She lies before me, naked, and I can't help but ache for

more.

"Well, I think we got our money's worth out of the room, huh?" she jokes, looking around the bed.

I raise my eyebrows. "I'm just getting started."

Crawling back onto the bed, I trail kisses up her body until I meet her sweet lips. Taking her hand in mine, I kiss each knuckle. I can only hope each kiss leaves a hot flame in its place, reminding her of what she does to me.

chapter
EIGHT

Aundrea

"You signed?" I hold the phone away from my ear as Genna's voice goes up an octave.

"Yep! Polly, our coordinator, faxed the contract over on Monday. We looked it over and faxed it back this morning. I just have to transfer the down payment."

"Dre! This is so exciting! When are you going to tell Mom? Should we call her now?"

"Calm down, lady." I laugh at her eagerness. I love how supportive my family is. "We're going to tell both sets of parents once we've actually met with a surrogate and have a good match."

"When do they think they'll have someone for you?"

"Polly seemed hopeful we would find someone within six months." Genna heaves a sigh. "Six months isn't *that* long. Besides, it can take longer than that to conceive the typical way." I hate using the term "normal" so Parker suggested using "typical" and it feels much better. For all intents and purposes, Parker and I *are* your typical couple. We just have to do things a little differently.

"I know. I only want this to move quickly for you."

"Eh, slow is good."

"Why?"

"I don't know." I shrug. "It gives us time to get settled into the new place, my job, save money, prepare. You know, all the basics."

"True."

"So, what time do you need us over tomorrow for these shenanigans of yours?" We finally nailed down a date to get together for her taste-testing dinner party. Jean has some business to do here in Rochester tomorrow, so it worked out perfectly.

"Jean says she'll get into town around three if you want to come over then. Jason and Kevin will ride together and get here about five or so."

I process the times in my head. "That should work. I volunteer tomorrow morning, so I'll come over right after that."

"Perfect. If you drop Parker off tomorrow he can hitch a ride with the guys."

"Sounds good to me."

⁓⊙ ☉⁓

I give my hair a quick tease and pin a few long, blonde strands in place, allowing my heated curls to fall over my right shoulder.

Since my hair has grown back, I try to wear it in different styles every day. I've even become more accustomed to wearing make-up and taking more time with my wardrobe. I still wear leggings, because they're the most comfortable thing on the planet, but I've learned to love and respect fashion. I owe a lot to Jean and her ability to transform any closet.

The temperature is humid for early May. We had a record cold winter and spring has started strangely. It's like Mother Nature can't decide which season she wants to be.

Amy, Ethan, and I arrive at Genna's together, pulling into her driveway alongside Jean's car.

I don't knock; I walk right in, followed by Amy and a very excited Ethan, Avenger toys in hand. We slip off our shoes and follow the smells of chocolate and cinnamon into the kitchen.

"It smells incredible in here," I announce rounding the corner to the kitchen.

"Oh. My. Gosh. This kitchen is a chocolate addict's dream." I swear, Amy's eyes are the size of the dinner plates on the counter. She can't seem to tear her eyes away from the chocolate treats on the table.

Ethan runs right over, asking to have one.

"Of course, honey," Genna answers. She looks back at the two of us. "Dre, can you please take the last of the truffles out of the oven?"

She doesn't waste any time. "How are you, Aundrea? Great, thanks for asking. Oh, by the way, can you please help me?" I tease, putting on oven mitts.

Amy snorts and steals a ball of gooey chocolate goodness with powder sugar dusted on top.

"I'm sorry. I just don't want them to burn. How are you?" She's kneading something on the counter that already looks good and it's not even cooked.

I laugh. "I'm good."

Amy moans, her eyes rolling back in her head. "Genna, this is … I now know why you've started your own business. This tastes like heaven." She takes another bite and adds, "And I love the new kitchen!"

Genna beams. "Thank you! Is Brandon coming?"

"Yeah, he'll be here soon. He was stuck in traffic so we hitched a ride with Dre."

With the truffles safely out of the oven, I take off the mitts. *My job is done.* "Where're Jean and Hannah?"

"Hannah is taking a late nap and Jean took a call from Kevin. I guess they're fighting." She rolls her eyes. I can't help but laugh.

I talked to Jean a couple days ago and she went on and on about how Kevin won't drop the topic of them taking things to the "next level." I'm learning that Jean has bigger commitment issues than I ever had.

Amy sits at the counter, taking in the mess. My eyes follow. "What else do you need help with?"

"I have a bottle of wine in the garage fridge. Can you grab it?"

"Of course, I can always find time to get wine!" From the garage, I call back, "How are you going to do all this on your own in a couple weeks?"

"I don't know yet. You sure you don't want to work with me?"

Bottle in hand, I walk back into the kitchen. "Not particularly. Food and me … well, you know."

"I've heard all about Dre's cooking," Amy speaks. "Which is why Parker cooks or she orders out when Brandon and I come over."

Genna laughs.

I shrug. "What can I say? Cooking is *not* my strength."

"True."

"But, I mean, if you need help setting up or delivering, I'm your gal."

I look at the label of the wine I'm holding. The Chocolate Shop: The Chocolate Lover's Wine.

"They make chocolate wine?"

"Yeah." She shrugs. "I was looking for something different for an after dinner drink and found that. I figured we should try it to see if it's any good."

"Yes, yes we should!" I say, gleeful.

Genna laughs as she chops apples and piles them in the cinnamon and sugar-filled dough. "I think I even saw a whipped cream flavored wine. I almost got it, but didn't."

I take out my phone to send Parker a quick text. I'm sure he's still seeing his animal patients, but he'll check it when he can.

Me: *Did you know they make chocolate flavored wine?*

My phone vibrates in my hand immediately.

> Mr. Handsome: *No, sounds good though.*

> Me: *It does! They also make a whipped cream flavor.*

> Mr. Handsome: *I want whipped cream.*

> Me: *Me too!*

All I can picture is strawberries with whipped cream and a little sugar. Yum!

> Mr. Handsome: *On you.*

Oh, boy.

> Me: *That sounds … interesting.*

> Mr. Handsome: *More specifically, I want to lick it off of you.*

> Me: *Oh …*

My chest buzzes with electricity and my cheeks burn. I look over at Genna, who is rolling up the apple dumplings, not paying me any attention.

> Mr. Handsome: *I want you to say that as I'm licking you clean.*

> Me: *Parker …*

> Mr. Handsome: *Yes, call out my name.*

Every nerve ending in my body is buzzing.

Me: *Stop it!*

Mr. Handsome: *Not until you're clean.*

Me: *LOL! You're so dirty.*

Mr. Handsome: *You don't know how dirty I can be.*

Me: *I bet I do.*

Parker: *Wanna bet?*

Do I? Yes, I do. This is one bet I *want* to lose.

Me: *I'll call and raise you two orgasms.*

Mr. Handsome: *It's on, woman. Tonight.*

My stomach flips. I bite my lip, doing my best not to smile.

"What has your panties dripping wet?" Jean asks, walking into the kitchen.

"Ethan, why don't we go get your shoes so you can run around in the backyard? I can watch you from the window," Amy says hurriedly.

He jumps down from his chair and skips to the front door. Amy follows and Jean gives her a remorseful smile, but Amy waves it off. Once they're out of view my head snaps to Jean.

"What are you talking about?"

Her eyes laugh. "Oh, please. I know sexting when I see it."

"Oh, I wasn't … we weren't …" I stammer, locking my phone and setting it on the counter.

"Riiight. The blush on your cheeks and the wicked smile

that you're badly trying to hide means nothing."

"Are you sexting in my kitchen when you're supposed to be helping me?"

"Uhh …"

"You were!" Jean shrieks.

"No!"

"Chocolate wine got you *that* excited?" Genna teases.

"What chocolate wine?" Jean asks, looking around.

"Here," I say.

"This looks yummy. Let's open it," Jean exclaims, taking it out of my hands.

"Not until after dinner. You need to have the full meal first and see if that's a good way to end the night," Genna explains.

"Well, according to Aundrea, it's a perfect way to end the night, if it gets you all hot and bothered." Jean gives me a wink and elbows me.

I can only manage an eye roll.

"Oh, come on. Give up the goods, Dre," she adds.

Ignoring her, I get comfortable at the counter and Jean eventually joins me. We sprinkle the last of the cinnamon and sugar on top of the dumplings before Genna puts them in the oven.

Hannah starts crying. Genna wipes her hands and goes to get her.

"You going to tell me what's going on with you and Kevin?" I ask now that we're alone.

Jean lets out a sad sigh and her shoulders slump a little.

"He wants me to leave Minneapolis and move here—or, rather, move in with him."

"And this is a problem why?"

"Because he doesn't understand that I have a job—one that I love, mind you—and I can't just pick up and leave for Rochester. What would I do here?"

I take a sip of Genna's water that looks lonely sitting on the counter. I'm not one to give relationship advice.

"The same thing you're doing now," Genna states,

walking back into the kitchen with Hannah in her arms.

"Sure, easy for you to say. Do you know how hard it is to find a job in my field?"

"Um, no I don't, considering I work with kids and food, not fashion." Genna laughs.

"Have you looked to see what's out there? This is a big city. You may be surprised at what you find," I add. It would be nice to have her close to me. "Besides, you're here now on business."

"Yes, but what I'm doing here isn't *really* business. It's talking to a few local boutiques about expanding and marketing. I was just helping out because it got me to come back and visit. And, no, I haven't looked for jobs. I told him he was crazy, and that I love him, but I love my career more," she huffs.

"Jean!"

"Oh, come on. I said it nicer than that."

Jean isn't one to get serious. She loves three things in life: fashion, men, and sex. Honestly, I'm surprised she's been with Kevin this long. Well, I'm sure I can guess why, but I'd rather not picture that part of his body. Regardless, I love that she's happy in her weird, twisted world.

"I can't believe you said that to him." I shake my head in disbelief.

"In the words of Brooke Davis 'clothes over bros.'"

I look at her with confusion. "Who is Brooke Davis?"

"*One Tree Hill.*" Her tone makes me think I should know what that is. "On the CW? Oh, come on! You've never watched that show?"

Genna and I look at each other and shake our heads. Laughing, I say, "No."

"It's on Netflix. Watch it." It's an order, not a request.

Amy comes back as the oven starts beeping and I jump up to get the trays, but Genna stops me. "I'll finish up if you can hold her." She hands me my sweet little niece and I'm settling back in at the counter the quiet is interrupted by loud, deep voices in the entryway. *The boys.*

Kevin walks in first. He gives me a small nod before walking over to Jean. She gives him a big welcoming hug and kiss. I've never questioned Kevin's feelings for my best friend. He treats her right, makes her smile, and loves her unconditionally. I wish she'd get over her own fear of commitment.

Jason comes over and takes Hannah from me. "How's my little girl this afternoon?"

"I'm good. Oh, you meant that little girl," Genna jokes.

When Parker enters our eyes find each other immediately. "Hello, handsome. You got out early. How'd you manage that one?" He's on call, so I was expecting him to show up a little late.

He pulls me close, kissing my temple. "It pays to be the boss."

"How are you?"

"Better now that I'm here. Although, I'd much rather be at home collecting on this bet."

I chuckle against his shoulder. "Is that so?"

"Yes," he says, his breath ghosting my ear. Leaning down, he nibbles at my earlobe. "I even picked up some whipped cream on the way over."

I exhale quickly. "Well, then …" Moving out of his grasp, I look at his face. "Let's make this an early night?"

"You've read my mind."

Brandon comes in about ten minutes later with Ethan in his arms.

Genna sits us down and she brings over the food. As she introduces each dish, she explains that she wants us to rate them on presentation and taste. I almost feel like I'm a judge on *Iron Chef*.

The room smells amazing, and the aroma gets stronger with each dish she puts in front of me. Over the next hour, we sample over a dozen different dishes. They're so good I pray she has more for us to take home.

When I excuse myself to go to the bathroom I check my phone for the first time since texting with Parker. I have two missed calls from Circle of Life and one voicemail. It's from Polly, asking for me to call her back.

I look at the time. Just after 5:30. I debate calling back this late, unsure if the clinic is still open, but decide to try anyway, redialing as I walk into the living room.

"Circle of Life, this is Heather, how can I help you?"

"Hi, my name is Aundrea Jackson. I'm returning Polly's call if she's still available?"

"Let me see if she's still here. Can you hold a minute?"

"Yes." I hope she is. It will drive me crazy wondering what it was about." I wonder if we missed something on the paperwork?

"Hello, Aundrea. Thanks for calling back," Polly says politely.

"No problem. Sorry I missed your calls. Is everything okay?"

"No worries, and yes, everything's fine. I wanted to catch you because we've found you a potential match."

Say again.

I fall onto the couch, stunned.

"Um … uh … excuse me?"

"I know this is a big surprise. Trust me, I'm equally surprised, but we had a surrogate whose contract ended up falling through early this morning. I want to be clear: it was nothing on her end. She's great and quite sad about the contract ending. The intended parents decided to wait a while longer."

"Um …"

"The thing is, Aundrea, she's ready to go. Her implantation was set to take place next Friday. She's started on the drugs to prepare her uterus and if we miss that window, you'll have to wait another month. Of course, that's fine, too. But if you and Parker are interested in next Friday, we'd have to move fast."

"Um …" *Wow.* "Wait, aren't there, like, other families ahead of us, waiting?" As much as I want this to be for us, I also can't help but wonder about all the other families that signed up before us.

"Yes, of course, but we work with locations and compatibility. We have IPs—intended parents—that come to us from all over the state requesting surrogates in different locations, but the surrogates also have a desired location. We have many families, but none that currently match Wendy's profile. She's in St. Paul, requesting to be with a family within one hundred miles. That's you and Parker."

"Oh, wow."

"I know this is a lot sooner than discussed, but she's the one, Aundrea. She's the match for you and Parker. As I said, though, I understand that you two may want to wait a while. I know you were expecting longer to prepare."

Wait a while? I don't think that's an option for us.

"No! Just give me a minute, please. I need to talk to Parker." I can't pass this opportunity up. At least, not without talking to Parker. *Shit, is it hot in here?* It's hot in here.

I fan myself with my hand. When that does nothing, I take a throw pillow from the couch and use it as a fan.

The room starts spinning. Or, maybe it's my head. I can't be sure. This is happening so much faster than we'd anticipated.

"I understand. Why don't you call me in the morning and let me know what your thoughts are? If you want to proceed, I'll set up a meeting with Wendy. If you want to wait a while longer, that's okay too. I'll be here until noon."

"No … um, I don't think we want to wait." *Do we?* "I'll talk to Parker and call you right back."

We hang up and I can't move.

"Aundrea?" Parker asks concerned. "You okay?"

I will my brain to send a signal to my mouth to speak, but it doesn't work. I'm still too shocked. My fingers begin to shake.

He sits next to me. "Babe?"

Turning a little, I meet his worried gaze. Behind him is an alarmed Genna.

"They found us a match." It comes out as barely a whisper.

"I'm sorry? What?"

"Circle of Life," I say louder, clearing my throat.

Parker breathes a sigh of relief next to me. "You mean?"

"Yeah. She's ready to go. Next Friday. I guess her contract with the intended parents fell through and we're a match. Polly wants to know if we want to proceed now, or wait a month ... or longer, if we're not ready."

"I don't want to wait."

"I don't think ..." *Fuck, spit it out!* "I don't think I want to wait either." It's the truth. As fast as this happening, I don't want to put it off. "Let's set up the appointment to meet her."

Holy shit!

"When did she say we could meet her?"

"She said she'd call her in the morning and set something up once we told her our decision."

He takes my phone.

"What are you doing?"

"We don't want to wait, right?"

"Right."

"Then I'm calling her back and telling her to set up the appointment. We'll make it work."

I don't even hear what Parker says to Polly.

I feel weightless. A tingling sensation begins to creep over me and I can't be sure if this is a dream or reality. Thinking about Parker and me having a baby brings such a feeling of wholeness. It's as if everything around me has come to a halt and nothing else matters. It's the one dream I've never thought could be possible, and it's simply astonishing that I've found someone who wants to give me that dream.

"We meet her Thursday," Parker says calmly, ending the call.

Someone else in the room sighs with relief. Genna's standing next to the couch, her eyes closed and her lips quivering.

I forgot she was even here.

When she opens her eyes and looks down at me there are tears trailing down her cheeks. Her eyes are soft. "Dre ..."

She trails off. But she doesn't need to finish. I know what her unspoken words are.

My bottom lip quivers as I try to hold back my own tears.

"We're going to have a baby!" Parker says, scooping me up and pulling me into his lap. "That was fast."

"I know."

"This is happening, Aundrea."

"I know." You'd think I could come up with something better to say.

I wrap my arms around his neck. "Parker, this means if it all works out we're doing the implantation in a week."

"We'll do it. We'll make it work. Whatever we have to do, come up with, sign, we'll do it. There's no question, babe."

My eyes shift over his shoulder to see Amy standing off to the side. She doesn't say anything, but her presence gives me all the reassurance I need.

I tuck my face into the crook of Parker's neck. *Whatever we have to do.*

As long as we do it together.

chapter NINE

Aundrea

Love illuminates life. There are different kinds of love, and only a select few are fortunate enough to experience every kind. I've been told there is no other love like the love a mother has for her child. It's deep, instant, and can never be broken. I knew if there was going to be anyone more excited about Parker and me having a baby than we were, it would be my mom.

I was going to hold back from telling her at least until we met with Wendy later today, I'm too excited when she calls.

"I—I don't understand. What do you mean?"

"We're having a baby, Mom."

"No, I get that. But ... how?"

I laugh. "A surrogate."

She's silent.

"Are you still there?"

"Yes, sorry. I'm ... shocked, that's all."

"In a good way?"

"Yes! Yes, of course, honey. I just didn't know you two were considering the idea, that's all."

"Well, Parker brought it up and, after a lot of thought, we decided we're ready."

"Are you?"

Come again? "Huh?"

"Sorry, what I mean is, with everything else that's going on? I want you to have a baby, Dre, don't get me wrong. I want you to have everything. I just … I guess I need confirmation that you're okay. That everything is going well with the routine visits, and that, from a health standpoint, you're okay to have a baby right now."

I take a deep breath and slowly exhale. "There's no need to worry."

"I'm your mother. It's my job to worry. I just want to be sure that your heart can handle the stress right now."

"Stress?"

"With a new house, graduation coming up, starting the new job. Add a newborn and money into that equation and it can be stressful."

My heart stops. I can feel it shutting down slowly. I feel a sharp pain, as if her hand reached through the line into my chest and is squeezing my heart.

Breathe, Aundrea. Breathe.

Inhale, exhale. Inhale, exhale.

Why does everything in my life have to come back to my health? Why does everything I do have to come with a constant reminder of my past, even at a happy time like this?

I try not to think about my past often. I take three pills daily for my cardiomyopathy, see Dr. James every three months, and have routine EKGs, echocardiograms, and any other imaging or bloodwork he feels is necessary. I also meet with my oncologist, Dr. Olson, every four months for a routine checkup, which won't stop until I'm put into remission in two years, and have routine labs for *her* necessary tests.

Everything is going fine.

"Mom, my health is under control. Really, there's no need to worry. Parker and I've discussed this and we're ready. *I'm* ready. I'm doing well and there is nothing holding us back."

"I know, honey. I only worry for you. I want nothing but the best for you two." Her voice cracks slightly.

I smile. "I know, Mom. Trust me when I tell you everything will be okay. It always works out."

"I know, bu—"

My phone beeps and I see that Amy's calling. "Mom, I have to let you go. I'll call you this week, okay?"

"Okay."

"Hey," I answer as I switch calls.

"Uh oh, what's the matter?" Amy asks.

"You saved me from my mother."

"Oh, man. Mothers." Her tone is sarcastic, but light. "What's the matter?"

"I told her about finding a surrogate."

"Yeah?"

"And she's concerned about the stress and timing of everything. I told her she doesn't have to worry and everything is okay, but, you know …"

"Dre, she's just concerned for you. She's your mother and she wants what's best."

"I know. It's … it's just that I was so excited to tell her. She's happy for us; I believe that. I know she wants me to have everything in life. But then she hit me with …"

"Reality."

"Kind of. Yeah."

"I get it. But, Dre, I'm a mom. Moms will always worry. We'll always have our child's best interest at heart. She's just making sure you two have thought this through. Trust me, she was probably like this with Genna too."

We both laugh. "You're probably right. Actually, I remember the conversation between Genna and my mom when she told her about the kitchen remodel. My mom didn't understand why she and Jason would consider that while she was still pregnant."

"See? She's only doing her job." Thank goodness for Amy.

"Thank you."

"Any time."

"Now, what's up with you?"

"I've been meaning to tell you: with the end of the school year coming, I've taken on some volunteering at Ethan's school, for their summer programs."

"Cool!"

"Yeah, Ethan's really excited that I'll get to spend more time with him, but that means my volunteering at Mayo will have to fluctuate."

"Oh …"

"I know. I'm not sure what my days will be at the school, so I'm not sure if we'll be together some weeks."

"It's okay. I understand."

"I was looking forward to more time with you before your job starts."

"Amy, honestly, it's okay. Family first. Isn't that what you always say? Seriously, don't worry about it. It's not like we won't see each other."

"You're an angel. Coffee soon?"

"Wouldn't miss it."

Parker walks over to me indicating we have to go. We say our goodbyes and pick a time to meet up.

"You ready?" he asks, wrapping his arm around my waist and kissing my temple.

"I was born ready."

"Then let's go meet the woman who's going to help bring our child into the world."

∼❀∽

I've lived a life that would make anyone afraid. Afraid of life, love—even hope. There is nothing I've faced that I didn't think I could overcome. Until now …

When we cross into the city, nausea washes over me, settling into the pit of my stomach. The restaurant isn't too far into St. Paul and the second it comes into view I feel as if I'm going to throw up. My hands are clammy and I'm starting to sweat. Running my fingers through my hair, I try to brush away the uneasy feeling that is taking over.

I've been nervous more times than I can count, but nothing like the feeling I have now. I'm afraid of disappointing the person who matters more to me than life itself. If there were ever a time to make a good first impression, this is it. This is the moment that could decide our future. That means it's also the moment that could push our happy ending further away.

When we pull into the parking spot we both remain silent. Parker's hands clutch the steering wheel, knuckles turning white.

I rest one hand on top of his. His grip loosens, but he doesn't look at me.

I flip down the visor to glance in the mirror. Suddenly, I feel like my eye make-up is too dark, my foundation is too thick, and my blush is too bright.

"You look great, Aundrea," Parker says, facing me.

I give him a weak smile. "Thanks, but I think I went a little overboard."

"Nonsense. You look amazing, as always. She's going to love you."

"Us. She's going to love us," I correct. I pray that I like her too. I'm terrified our personalities won't click, and we'll decide we're not a good match.

"Ready?" Parker asks.

My hand stays on top of his.

"What if it doesn't work out?" I choke.

"Aundrea, I won't stop until we have a baby in our arms. If this match doesn't work, there will be another one. I assure you."

I nod. I need the reassurance. I just want this to work out. Slowly, I get out of the car, trying to keep myself together. Meeting Parker at the front of the car, I wrap my arm around his waist as we walk toward the front door. I take slow, deep breaths, trying to control my nerves. My dress feels too short all of a sudden. I knew I should have gone with the longer one.

"Stop fidgeting."

"I shouldn't have worn this. It's too short, and cut a little low. My boobs are practically bursting out."

Parker looks down at my cleavage. "Nope, looks great." He winks, then waggles his eyebrows.

I roll my eyes. "You're such a man."

"Last I checked."

Chuckling, I push into his side playfully. I like that he can make light of the moment, sensing my nervousness.

"I'm serious, Parker."

"So am I."

"No, I mean it. I want to look good. I don't want her to think I'm trashy."

Parker stops mid-stride. He tilts my chin up so I'm looking directly at him. "Listen to me. You do not look trashy. You're beautiful. The dress was a perfect choice, and your make-up looks great."

"Thank you."

He gives me another wink before taking my hand back into his.

"And for the record, I can't wait to get you home, flip up your dress, and bury myself deep inside of you."

"Parker!"

He shrugs, smiling. "What? It's the truth."

"I can't believe you're thinking about sex right now when we're about to meet the woman who's potentially going to be carrying our child."

"Honey, I'm *always* thinking about sex with you. Besides, I'm trying to calm you down so you stop fidgeting," he whispers as we walk through the door.

"I'm not," I hiss back.

I'm totally fidgeting. I can't stop fiddling with my dress, rolling the fabric between my fingers. I start rocking side to side as we wait for the hostess. No matter what I try, I can't stay still.

When she returns, Parker explains that we're meeting someone and gives her Wendy's name. She walks us toward the back of the restaurant.

My heart quickens, seeming to beat twice as fast as it did a second ago. My breathing slows down, and I'm pretty sure I can't hear anything around me except the pulse throbbing in my neck. It's almost like being in a slow motion scene in *The Matrix*. I can see people's mouths moving, but can't hear anything.

Fortunately, by the time we reach a small table in the back, my hearing cuts in. "Here you are," the hostess says, leaving Parker and me standing awkwardly in front of two strangers.

"Hi!" the woman practically yells, standing. "I'm Wendy." She holds out her hand. "This is my husband Ron."

She's of medium height and doesn't look older than thirty. Her light golden hair is pulled back into a ponytail and her bangs have a slight curl. She's very pretty and her husband is equally attractive.

Parker shakes hands with her and Ron, introducing himself, then me. "Hello," I manage to get out, shaking her cold hand.

"Please, sit down." She gives us a reassuring smile.

I take the inside seat, resting my knee against the wall in an attempt to keep it from bouncing.

"So, Wendy, what do you do for work?" Parker asks.

I'm glad he breaks the ice first; I'm not sure I can speak.

"I'm a nurse."

Ron gives a proud smile.

"Wow, that's awesome," I say, finding my voice.

"Thanks." She beams. "I love it."

"How long have you been doing that?" Parker inquires.

"About six years now. I work in orthopedics. What do you two do?"

"I'm a veterinarian."

"And I'm graduating college in a few weeks." I feel a little awkward saying that—being twenty-four and discussing having a baby when I'm still in school.

"Starting in September, Aundrea will be working in astrophysics."

"That's awesome; congrats."

"Thank you."

Our waitress comes over and we tell her we need a minute to look over the menu, but none of us do. No one speaks. We stare awkwardly at one another, waiting for someone to make the first move.

Ron clears his throat and Wendy must take that as her cue to keep the conversation going.

"Is that how you two met? Through the clinic?" she asks.

We look at one another. Parker winks and my heart skips a beat.

"Kind of." I laugh uncomfortably.

Parker takes my hand. "I worked with her brother-in-law, who hired her. We met a few days before she started working, but it took some convincing on my part to get her to go on a date with me."

"The hockey game wasn't a date."

"Like I said, call it what you will; it was a date."

I shake my head, but laugh internally. After all these years, you would think we'd have that cleared up.

"What a fun story! I love it."

If she only knew.

Parker clears his throat. "What made you decide to be a surrogate?"

"I did this for my sister two years ago. She tried to have a baby and couldn't. They really wanted their own and I offered. It was so amazing to be able to give that gift to them. I told Ron I'd love to do this for a family I didn't know. It took until about four months ago for us to decide it was a good time to do it. I was surprised to be matched so soon, but then …"

Ron stays quiet, but takes her hand in support. I can tell how hard it was on her for the previous contract to fall through. She seems to really want to do this for a deserving couple.

"I'm sorry that fell through," I say. Though Polly told me it was the intended parents who called it off, we're not allowed to discuss details with Wendy per the legal contract.

"Me too, but, like you said, we're here now. One's loss is another's gain," Parker states.

Wendy smiles.

"You know, this *is* an amazing gift. It takes a strong, generous person to be able to do this for someone. Twice," I say.

"Thank you. It was the most rewarding thing I've ever done for another person. I can't tell you how great it felt knowing I was helping my sister fulfill her dream of having a child. I would love to do that for another family. I thought I found them, but they decided they weren't ready. Which is okay. I know firsthand how scary it is to have a child and the nerves that take over. I don't blame them. I'm just grateful Polly found you two so quickly, and I hope it works out."

She's so nice and I can't help but like her right away.

The waitress returns and we order. I don't think any of us can handle eating much. I take a small sip of my water before asking, "How many kids do you have?"

"Two. Both girls."

"And you look *that* good!" I say. She really does.

Wendy flushes at my compliment.

"How old are they?" Parker asks.

"Seven and five. My niece is two now. It was hard for my sister to watch me get pregnant with them so easily. She and my brother-in-law tried for eight years. She took every fertility drug you could think of. Nothing was working, and the doctors couldn't explain why she wasn't getting pregnant. A medical mystery they called it."

"Wow," Parker and I say. I feel awful for her sister. I can't imagine trying that long for a baby only to be let down month after month. I also give her a lot of credit. It takes a strong woman to go through all that for so long.

"May I ask you how long you've been trying?" Wendy says.

I look over at Parker. This is the moment I was dreading. I've never liked being the center of attention.

Parker starts to answer for me, knowing how I feel, but I know I should be the one to explain. "I'm a cancer survivor. Unfortunately, I'm not able to carry a child." I say, as honestly and firmly as I can. It takes a lot to open up and say you have cancer, but it shouldn't take a lot to say you are a survivor.

And that's what I am.

A survivor.

Parker takes my hand in his and I can feel him trying to comfort me.

"Wow, I'm so sorry to hear that, but congratulations," Wendy says. She looks like she wants to reach out and touch me, too; her eyes are sorrowful and I can tell her heart goes out to us.

Ron gives me a sad smile and echoes Wendy. "I'm sorry to hear that, but I'm glad everything is on the positive now."

"Thank you. Really, it's okay. There's no need to be sorry. I've been cancer-free for almost three years now."

"That's something to be proud of right there."

"It is, thank you."

I don't feel it's necessary to discuss my cardiomyopathy with her. She doesn't need to hear about how I couldn't catch a break. Telling her about my history is one thing; what might be in my future is quite another.

We eat lunch and continue talking for a few hours. We learn more about Wendy's deliveries and children, and about Ron, who works in construction. When it's time to go, we say our goodbyes and exchange hugs.

She's perfect. I can't find one thing I don't like about her. We get along great, she's smart, has a wonderful life, loves kids, and seems like she'll care for our unborn baby as if he or she were one of her own.

When we get back in the car, Parker and I start talking at the same time.

"She's perfect!"

"She's great, Aundrea. Her enthusiasm about the entire thing, and her reasoning … I couldn't ask for a better reason from someone."

"It's also comforting to deal with someone who has gone through this process before."

"I agree. I have a good feeling about this and her."

Parker gives me a long kiss filled with promise before we set off home. I refuse to let anyone or anything ruin this for us. Nothing else matters.

chapter
TEN

Parker

We drive back to Circle of Life to meet Polly. It didn't take much to get Kevin and Jason to cover my afternoon schedule. They're both very supportive of this entire process and told me not to worry. They'll cover when they can.

"Parker, Aundrea, this is Tim. He's going to be representing you. He'll walk you through the contract that we've started and will finalize after the numbers are figured out. Then he'll have the contract sent over to the lawyer who is representing Wendy. If she accepts, we'll proceed."

"Sounds good," I say as Aundrea nods frantically.

"Okay, let's get to it."

It seems so formal. Who would have thought that having a baby would mean so many formalities? This is way more invasive than I'd ever thought.

"Okay, first things first," Tim says, "I've drawn up the contract based on Wendy's previous contract that fell though. Remember, this is all negotiable." We both nod. "She's asking for $22,000. That is a little lower than the average rate of $25,000 for a single birth, so I think it's fair to stick with that."

Aundrea looks my way. I can see her processing this, but we knew from our paperwork to expect about $25,000, so that's a non-issue.

I run the numbers in my head. "And what happens if she doesn't get pregnant?"

"We'll write it into the contract that the first of four payments is non-refundable, with the stipulation that she agrees to try for four months. If she doesn't get pregnant in four months, she is free to walk away, as are both of you. Or you can re-sign and the initial payment will carry over for an additional two months. After six months, the contract is void and, if you wish to continue, new contracts will be signed."

"That sounds reasonable," Aundrea says.

"I like what you've suggested," I agree.

"Next up, there is no mention of how many embryos you want to transfer. Wendy is open to a maximum of two, but in the case of a multiple birth the $22,000 doubles."

Aundrea's eyes go wide. "Twins?"

"It's just a formality we must discuss," Tim says calmly.

"We didn't discuss how many," I add. I think we both assumed it would only be one.

"The number to be transferred is strictly up to you. Some people transfer up to four embryos for a higher probability of pregnancy, but Wendy is young and healthy, so the chances of one taking are higher than if she were older and higher risk," Polly interjects.

"One is good!" Aundrea says quickly. We all laugh.

"Okay, one it is," I declare. "And if by some chance that splits and turns into multiples, we'll make it work."

"Aundrea, are you okay?" Polly asks. I look over to see her gulping her water.

"This is a lot, I know, but we need to cover every eventuality so we're prepared," I reassure her.

"I understand. It all sounds good."

I squeeze her hand to let her know it's okay and don't let go as we discuss maternity leave, vaginal versus a caesarean deliveries, and other costs. We figure everything out to the last penny. Tom and Polly don't leave out a single detail. We spend three hours making sure we have the clearest, most airtight contract we can. I ask questions, make notes, and ask Aundrea's opinion on everything, which keeps her relaxed. But by the time we head home, Aundrea has yet to speak more than a few words.

She's staring out her window, clearly thinking hard about something. Her mouth is a straight line and she's twirling a strand of her silky hair around her finger.

Reaching over, I tap her leg. "Hey, you okay?"

When she looks at me it's like she's pulling herself out of a fog. "Yeah, sorry."

"What has you so deep in thought?" She licks her lips, then begins to play with her thumb ring. "Aundrea?"

"Do we really have this kind of money right now, Parker? For all this? I mean, with the house and all?" I can see the lines of concern on her face.

"We are more than okay, babe. I promise. And besides, I'd pay twice that amount if it meant having a baby with you."

Her lips tremble as she rests her head back. "Have you always been this perfect?"

"No. *You* make me perfect."

She closes her eyes, finally resting peacefully. "I love you," she says.

"I love you more, beautiful."

～♥ ♥～

Wendy accepted our contract Monday, which means everything needs to happen quickly. The embryos need three to five days to develop, so we decide to have the clinic fertilize eight eggs, one to be transferred now and the rest to be used at a later date if needed.

We arrive in Minneapolis just after 7:00 that evening. We're told to have the sample to the office no later than 8:00 Tuesday morning and given proper instructions on collecting it. They said I could deposit the sample at the clinic so we wouldn't have to come up a night early, but there is no way I'm ejaculating in a cup with nurses and doctors walking around just outside the door.

When morning comes, I think I must still be dreaming. I feel the softness of Aundrea's lips first, wrapping around me, followed by her warm breath. I become hard instantly when her tongue comes out, tracing around the tip of my erection. She swirls her tongue around the tip before taking me all the way into her mouth.

I groan out, "Holy, fucking shit, Aundrea." My eyes pop wide open as she takes me to the back of her throat, slowly easing me in and out several times.

"Fuck, Aundrea."

Her mouth feels so fucking amazing right now. As her head moves up and down, I tug gently on her hair. I don't force her to move faster, allowing her to go at the speed she pleases. She's amazing all on her own.

Letting out a sigh, I relax into the pillow.

She stops moving her head and starts tracing my hardness with her tongue, sucking and tasting every inch. I lose control, pulling on her hair, and she moans backs. The vibrations from her mouth set my insides on fire.

"That's it, baby," I cry out.

She pumps me fast as she sucks. It's the hottest thing ever, and I only wish there was a mirror above me so I could watch her every move.

As much as I'm enjoying this, there's nothing I want more than to get her off. The look on her face when she screams out my name is one of the hottest things I've ever seen. I know the minute I finish we'll have to head to the clinic, and I'm far from wanting to finish.

A glance at the clock shows that it's only about 6:30. *Plenty of time.*

Reaching down, I pull her up. She glances up at me in confusion. "What? Is everything okay?" She flushes with embarrassment. It's so sexy.

"You're perfect, but I want to—I *need* to get you off. I want to make you feel good, babe."

"Parker, this is supposed to be about you today. Not me."

"It's always about you." I flip her to her back, and she lets out a small squeal.

"Parker!"

"Trust me."

Pulling down her thong, it takes everything in me not to bury myself deep inside. She looks so tempting, but I know if I get inside her, I'll never be able to stop and finish in some fucking little cup.

I kiss her stomach, then down to her thigh and back up again. Her legs fall open, giving me all the access I need. I bring my mouth to the place I know is aching to be touched. That I am aching to touch. As soon as my tongue touches her she's calling out my name.

I lap at her slick folds, tracing circles, then dip down inside of her. Her breathing picks up and when her hands grip my hair, I move faster. I love when she pulls my hair.

I lift her legs up on my shoulders. As my tongue moves, her hips rock against me. I slip a finger inside her, too, and, as she cries out in surprise, I slide another finger inside, filling her. Her hips begin moving faster, riding my face as I thrust my fingers deeper.

"That's it baby," I murmur against her.

"Please, don't stop."

Sweat drips down my back and I welcome the heat in the room.

"That … don't … yes, like that," she moans as I move my tongue. There's nothing sexier than her telling me what she likes in bed.

It doesn't take long before I feel her body tighten around my fingers. I don't stop moving until her breathing slows and I know her last wave is over. Wiping my mouth on the inside of her thigh, I slide back up her body, trailing kisses as I go. She cups my face and presses our mouths together. I groan in response, pushing my tongue inside so she can taste her own sweetness. She cries out, clawing at me to move closer.

Sex has always been great with Aundrea. I've never had to question it, or ask for more, and I love that she doesn't shy away from me when I go down on her.

"Now, handsome, I have some work to do." Sliding out from underneath me, she goes back to her earlier position.

I glance at the clock to check the time: just after seven. I hate being on a schedule when it comes to this, but I also don't want to miss our opportunity.

We're about a five-minute drive from the clinic and it will only take fifteen minutes to shower and get ready, so that leaves us with a good twenty minutes. *More than enough time to get the job done.*

Aundrea's hot mouth is back on my erection, and I close my eyes with pleasure. She sucks hard, pumps fast, and doesn't stop until I'm close to my release.

My hands weave through her hair, gently coaxing her up and down. She doesn't need much coaxing. This woman knows exactly what she's doing with her mouth.

"Babe, cup. I'm close." She stops suddenly, reaching over to get the cup the clinic provided to us. I continue to stroke myself as I wait. I don't look away from her naked form, her back arching perfectly as she gets the cup.

With the lid off in record time, I lean up, spilling my release. Aundrea gives me a few soft kisses on the side of my face as I do.

"That was so romantic." I laugh.

She giggles, falling onto the bed next to me. She falls quiet when I cup her face tenderly, and a flush creeps over her checks. "God, you're beautiful."

The air between us heats up again.

chapter
ELEVEN

Aundrea

I drive to Olaf Café to meet Amy the Sunday following the implantation. It's a newer café in the heart of downtown Rochester, which is why I refuse to move from this city. This area has the best coffee and food. Period.

With only a few other cars in the parking lot, I spot Amy's Corolla easily. I walk quickly through the sprinkling rain. As nice as it was this morning when I opened the windows, I still love the rain. Especially on warm spring days like today. There's something about the brisk air mixed with the smell of rain hitting the asphalt that puts me in a good mood.

Moving past a middle-aged couple in the entryway, I shake off the rain.

"Good morning!" the hostess greets. I've seen her before. She's young, maybe eighteen or nineteen, and has this adorable pixie cut. It suits her features.

"Morning," I reply.

"How many?"

"Two, but I think the woman I'm meeting is already here."

"Right this way." We weave through the small seating area and past the electric fireplace that's glowing in the corner to the faint sound of alternative rock. The café has about fifteen tables inside and eight on the covered patio. On rainy days like today, I love nothing more than to come here, sit outside under the canopy, and listen to the sound of rain. It's relaxing and helps me think, so it's perfect that we're meeting here.

Amy looks tired, with dark circles under her eyes, but she smiles when we approach.

"Can I get you anything?" the hostess asks as I take my seat across from Amy. We're at my favorite table in the corner. It's perfect for people watching on the street outside. The rain is soft and light so it doesn't blow in our faces.

"Yes. I'll take a tall house blend with extra cream and sugar, please. Oh, and a water with lemon. Thank you." Even though I know the menu by heart, I look at it anyway.

"How are you?" I ask.

"I'm doing good. We stayed up way too late last night packing."

"Packing?"

"Yeah, Ethan and I are going to go spend some time up north with my parents. Just a week or so before the summer programs start."

"That will be fun!" I smile.

After a few minutes, she asks about Wendy. "You're in a good mood. I take it everything went well?"

I raise my eyebrows.

"You can't stop smiling."

I'm smiling? I grin even wider—until it's almost painful.

When I don't answer right away she says, "Spill it."

"Wendy's perfect. The implantation went so smoothly. She had to rest for the first day, but that was it."

"Dre! That's so exciting." She tears up.

"It's crazy that it's really happening!"

"What do you mean? You didn't think it would?"

"I thought we'd get some time to prepare. If I'm being honest, I'm a little freaked out." Not in a bad way. More like the exciting moment when you don't know whether you should be screaming at the top of your lungs, crying, or jumping for joy.

"I get it. It's a big step to take, but trust me, there's no better feeling in the world than when you meet your child for the first time—when they look up at you."

I want that feeling.

"Once I got my life back on my own timeline, I've been focused on having everything go as planned. It just goes to show you things never go the way you expect them to." I let out a small laugh.

"This wasn't in your plan?"

"It's not that having a child wasn't in our plan. I've wanted a family since the moment I was told I may never be able to carry my own children. I wanted to leave the doctor's office that day kicking and screaming I was so mad. Mad that I'd just learned I had cancer and needed all this treatment, and mad that something I hadn't really known I wanted, until that moment, was being taken away. First, I was in denial, but then it was pure anger. I figured that if I couldn't carry a child then I wouldn't freeze my eggs. I'd just adopt and be content with that."

"But you did freeze your eggs, and here you are all these years later getting ready to have your baby."

"I know. I just thought we'd get time to process it all; I don't think it's really sunk in yet. And then … you know, I told my mom about meeting with Wendy and she makes me start to think about …"

"What?"

I don't like talking about this. I hate feeling so weak. I feel like when I'm taking a step forward, I'm being pushed back down when I'm forced to think about it all.

"Dre?"

"All the what-ifs when it comes to my health. I've dreamed of this, Amy. And then … my mind plays tricks on me and I starting thinking, what if my heart isn't under control and everything spirals downward? Or … I go in for a scan and they find something? I could handle it. I know I could. I'm strong enough. But could Parker handle it? Then I think about our unborn baby and if *something* did show up one day, how would that affect my child?" I'm not sure if I'm making sense, but I need to express my thoughts.

"No, I'm stopping you right there. There are no what-ifs. There is no more cancer, Aundrea. That chapter of your life is over. Dre, listen to me. You've had to grow up much sooner than most people your age. Look at the last year alone, and how much you've grown. How confident you are, not only in your personal life but in the impact you have on people you see in the clinic every week. You're following your dreams, and I'm so proud of you."

I fight back tears. "Yes, it's been three years, but I have *two* more years until I'm considered in remission. That's a long time. Do you know what I go through every time I get a cold and have swollen glands? The first thing I think is that my cancer is back. I have to fight the urge to panic. Not because *I'm* scared, but because I think about how Parker will take the news. How he would hold up. And now …" I collect my jumbled thoughts, hoping to make sense of them.

"I'm not afraid of my cancer, my heart, or dying, Amy. I never was. But I'm terrified to leave my loved ones behind. I'm scared beyond belief to think about my child living without me, motherless. About how it will affect the rest of their life. That they'll have to go on without knowing who I am; that there are so many things I would miss out on. I never want to watch those around me suffer if I get diagnosed again, or if one day I get bad news about my heart."

"We're all going to die, Dre. You *will* leave your loved ones and there is no way around that. It may not be cancer, or your heart, but *something* will take your life one day, and when that day comes you better be screaming from the rooftops that you lived a life worth screaming over. The sooner you accept that, the sooner you'll be able to move forward with your life.

"I haven't met one person—me included—who hasn't thought about death and how it will affect the people they leave behind. But believe me when I tell you I will never let doubt or fear run my life. As cheesy as the saying is, I *will* cherish each day as if it's my last. You should do the same. Life's too short, Aundrea. Be happy in the now."

Her words hit me right in the pit of my stomach. *The sooner you accept that, the sooner you'll be able to move forward with your life.*

"I want that, but how do you get over your deepest fear and move on to live the life you want to have? That you *deserve* to have?"

"You look fear in the eye and jump off the ledge. Have you talked this over with Parker?"

I shake my head.

"Genna?"

"No. Genna's like my mom. She tends to worry, and I don't want that. She's in a really good place right now with the business, Jason, and Hannah. The last thing I want is to worry her with my random thoughts."

"What about Jean?"

"Jean knows. She's always known." Jean listens. She makes the pain go away with only her presence.

"Talk to her."

"I hate showing that I'm weak. I'm supposed to be strong."

"You are, but sometimes the strong ones need to lean on someone, too. You can't always be the one to make everything perfect. Your past doesn't determine who you are. Don't let it. You need to have faith. Getting over a fear doesn't happen overnight, but accepting it will get you a lot closer to being over it."

"You're right."

I need to continue doing what I have been: focusing on our future.

Our family's future.

"When I was diagnosed with breast cancer it made me reevaluate my life. I was so focused on having everything around me in line that I lost focus on what was right in front of me: my family." Amy pauses, sipping her water. "Just know that sometimes what life brings you—what's not in your control—can be positive."

I cradle the hot mug of coffee, focusing on how the warmth seeps into my fingertips and hands and moves through me. The aroma of the dark roast, with a hint of vanilla from their special creamer, fills the air.

"When did you become so wise?" I ask, smiling weakly.

Amy grins. "Don't dwell so much on your path having to go a certain way, Aundrea. There will always be bumps in the road, but sometimes those bumps are good. You'll see that when you're finally holding that precious gift in your arms, and I hope to see that day."

I always said during my cancer that life has a plan for me. Maybe the things you never thought you'd get to have, live to see, or be able to do somehow find you.

～♡ ♡～

"Aundrea Jackson," a loud, echoey voice crackles. "Graduating with honors, Aundrea is earning her Bachelors in Physics." I take a deep breath as I stand. The white honor ropes hang freely around my neck as I march to the stage where the dean of students is standing front and center.

It's been a week since the implantation, and no news yet. Not that either of us were expecting to hear something by now, but we're eager.

Looking into the crowd, I scan for my family and friends as I cross the stage. They're not difficult to find. My parents, Genna and Hannah, Jason, Jean, Kevin, and even Shannon from For the Love of Paws are all here. Unfortunately, Amy and her family couldn't make it.

My eyes land on Parker last. He towers over the rest of them so our gazes can meet and linger. His face is bright, his eyes glowing, and the most handsome smile I've ever seen is framed by light stubble.

"Congratulations," the dean says, pulling my attention

from Parker. He shakes my hand and moves on to calling the next name.

Whistling, clapping, and yelling erupt as I finish my walk across the stage. It's a miraculous feeling to finally take the steps. To be here.

I didn't get to graduate with my high school class, so crossing the stage today, surrounded by my friends and family, gives me a sense of feeling whole. Of finally achieving something I've worked so hard to accomplish.

I let out a deep breath as I look back at Parker's smile. He gives me a wink that sends my heart into a flurry, and I smile back.

We all have those moments when we stop and look back at our lives. When we think about all the things we've accomplished and the things that have lead us to where we are today. This is definitely one of mine.

I take my seat and watch the rest of the students cross the stage.

"I give you the graduates of Winona State University, Rochester," the dean thunders, and I flinch.

The auditorium fills with a loud roar as we throw our caps high in the air. The rambunctious audience's hoots and hollers bounce off the walls. I catch my cap in my hands, smiling at the thought of being a college graduate.

"Congratulations," Parker says when I jump into his arms after the ceremony. He twirls me in a circle, my black gown flowing in the wind.

"Thank you." When he sets me back on my feet, I'm instantly met with hugs and congratulations from the rest of my family.

"I'm so proud of you honey," my mom sniffles. Her eyes are red and swollen with emotion.

"Thank you, Mom."

"Come here, little girl." My dad pulls me into a tight hug. "I love you." He kisses the top of my head. "I'm so proud of the spitfire you are and the fact that you never let go of your dreams. I knew you could do it." His voice cracks on his last words and tears sting my eyes.

"Dad, I love you. I couldn't have done anything without your love and support. It gave me the strength to stand here today."

He wipes a tear. "This is just the beginning for you, baby girl."

I can't imagine what this feels like for my parents. I love knowing that I'm giving my parents a memory they'll never forget.

A memory I'll never forget.

Genna invited us all back to her place for a celebratory dinner. I think it's an excuse to get to use her new kitchen. Now that school's out, it's the only place she can be found.

I take a seat next to Shannon on the patio. We're all huddled around the crackling fire that Jason started.

"How's Wendy doing?" Shannon asks.

Just as I'm about to answer, Parker lets out a deep laugh. I take him in. He's wearing dark jeans and a blue pin-striped dress shirt with the sleeves rolled to his elbows. His head is tipped backward, mouth open, and he's holding his beer with both hands, the sweat on the bottle dripping onto the brick below. His laugh sends rumbles within my own chest.

He looks so sexy: laid back, comfortable, and happy.

Looking back at the girls, I smile. "She's good. We're waiting very anxiously."

"That's so exciting. And when are you moving into the house?"

"Next week."

"I don't know why more women don't do what you're doing," Jean announces.

"What do you mean?" Shannon asks.

"If there are women willing to carry a baby for someone, why don't more do that? I mean, come on. It's the best pregnancy ever. You don't gain any weight, you get to go about your life as usual, you don't have to go through all the sickness that's associated with pregnancy, and then *bam*, you bring home a baby."

"Personally, I'd hate that. I feel like it's a part of the female nature to carry a child. I can't imagine giving up the chance to feel them grow inside of you, moving around, to connect with them and know you're creating a life. I bet it's an amazing feeling. I'd hate to not experience—" Shannon stops speaking suddenly, looking at me. She claps a hand over her mouth, eyes intent. "Dre, I'm so sorry. That was inconsiderate of me. I can't believe myself. Shit." Her voice is muffled, but I make out the words clearly.

"Don't be; it's okay." I give her a reassuring smile. "I agree with you." At seventeen I was forced into a life I didn't want. A life no one wants. I'd love nothing more than to experience pregnancy, but I've had time to accept it, to become okay with not carrying my own child.

I have to be.

Aundrea

We roll into the early days of summer with no news from Wendy. The anticipation keeps growing and I'm not sure how much longer I can pass the time. Parker said we should call, but I can't bring myself to do it yet. It's been almost three weeks since the implantation and I'm terrified to hear that it didn't take.

I don't think I'm prepared for that.

Pushing the double doors open, I enter For the Love of Paws. Parker had an early meeting and left before me this morning. It's my second day back working here and everyone has been welcoming.

When I reach Shannon's desk, she's laughing. "Somebody's in trouble," she sings as she staples some papers together, not looking at me.

"Excuse me?"

She nods toward Parker's office.

Confused, I set my purse down and walk to Parker's office.

The clinic is split into two. The left half is the regular clinic and the right half is the emergency clinic where there are three exam rooms and two procedure rooms. With the expansion came new staff, who I get along with well.

Parker's office is my favorite in the entire building. I helped him pick out all the furniture and artwork. He even had a built-in bookshelf and a comfortable couch put in for me so I'd never have a reason not to visit.

His office door is slightly ajar and I can hear him talking. "Yes, that's perfect. Yeah, that would be great, and don't forget to —. Okay, good."

Knocking softly, I push open the door to find Parker sitting in his big black leather chair behind his almost-too-large-for-the-room cherry wood desk. He motions me in.

"Hey, I don't mean to cut this short, but Aundrea just walked in," he says. "Just let me know what I owe you. Thanks. You too, bye." Hanging up, he stands and walks over. "Good morning."

"Hi."

He pulls me into his arms before I can even ask how he's doing. He kisses the top of my head, then releases me.

"You do know you're late, correct?" He looks at his watch. "Start time is 8am, Mrs. Jackson. You're twenty-five minutes late." His face is stern, with no signs that he's joking, and I laugh internally.

I pout. "I'm sorry, Dr. Jackson. Please don't write me up."

Leaning down, his lips brush along the shell of my ear. "I'm not going to write you up; however, I don't have a problem with showing you a little discipline." I suck in a sharp breath. His eyes dart over my shoulder and he quickly steps away. "Now, get to work. I expect my employees to start on time." His words come out annoyed and I can only laugh at his bossy behavior.

As I turn to walk away I hear him say softly, "We'll discuss your discipline later, when we're at home." I look over my shoulder to see his wicked grin.

Shannon shakes her head when I see her. "I tried to warn you."

"I'm not worried. That man has nothing on me." I take my seat behind the desk next to her. She laughs.

My computer isn't even turned on when my cell starts to ring with the new Sia song that Genna set as my ringtone. I fumble with my phone, trying to silence it. I'm about to put it back in my purse when I notice the name displayed across the front.

"Wendy, hi! How are you?"

Shannon's head snaps to me. I guess that was a little loud. I mouth "Sorry," and turn my focus back to Wendy.

"Hi. I hope it's not too early to call you?"

"Of course not."

"Okay, good." I hear the relief in her voice. "Are you two settled into the new house yet?"

"We closed yesterday and are moving in this week."

"Awesome!" She makes some small talk, and I'm trying to reciprocate, but I can feel the sweat forming under my arms. I hate small talk. I want to press her about the baby.

"Is everything okay with you?" I ask.

"Everything's good. The reason I'm calling is because I took a pregnancy test."

Really? You're going to stop there and leave me hanging? "And?" I sit up taller.

"It was positive."

Once the words leave her mouth I can't speak. I wait for something to come out, but nothing does.

"Hello? Are you still there?"

"Positive!" I scream.

Shannon jerks, sending papers sliding off her desk. An exam room door opens and Kevin pops his head out. "Everything okay out here?"

"Yes, sorry!" I wave him off, grinning.

"Yes," Wendy whispers. A small sniffle comes through the line. "I wanted to let you know that you're going to be a mom." Her voice cracks on the last word.

My lip begins to tremble and tears fill my eyes, then slide down my cheeks. Shannon's watching me intently and I can sense she knows what's going on.

We're going to have a baby.

I want this more than I've ever wanted anything in my entire life. Something I didn't think I'd ever truly get to experience is happening. I knew I wanted a baby, but hearing Wendy tell me I'm going to be a mom is one of the best, most surreal moments of my life, and I don't know how I ever questioned that this was the right time. I know how Genna felt when she found out she was pregnant with Hannah, and how excited I was for her, but to actually experience that feeling myself is unlike anything I've ever experienced or witnessed.

Wendy's crying a little, but she says, "I'm so happy for you two."

"Thank you so much, Wendy. For everything. You don't know how much this meant to me. To us. I will forever be grateful for what you're giving Parker and me. You've just given us the best news imaginable." I end the call after making plans for us to get together soon.

Shannon starts speaking a mile a minute. Everything comes out so fast all I can make out is, "Congratulations."

I'm wiping my eyes when Parker's deep voice interrupts us. "Mrs. Jackson, do I need to remind you what the employee handbook says about the use of cellular devices during working hours?"

I look from Shannon to the phone still in my hands. I shake my head, my answer a barely audible, "No."

Composing myself, I glance his way. His face is one hundred percent serious. I look away. I feel hot and flushed with all the excitement. Parker looks between Shannon and me and I can see the smile he's trying to hide.

"Good."

Pushing off the counter, he walks away. When he's about to round the corner again he stops, turning back to me. "Don't let me catch you on your phone again. I'd hate to have to take action." He leaves me to ponder his words.

"Take action?" I mock. "Like what? Fire me?"

Shannon laughs. "That man looked like he wanted to light a fire all right."

"Oh, shut it." I giggle.

"That man has it bad for you."

I nod.

"Why didn't you tell him, Dre?"

"He caught me off guard."

"Well, go after the boss man!" she yells, scooting my chair forward.

I move quickly, almost skipping the halls to his office. When he's not there I go to the lounge.

"Sorry about earlier," he says, standing up when he sees me enter.

"For threatening me?"

"Threaten? I didn't threaten."

"I'd hate to have to take action," I mock in my best Parker voice.

"Is that what I sound like?"

"Yes."

He laughs the deep, throaty laugh I love to hear. "I needed to sound authoritative. Did it work?" He's grinning from ear to ear.

I shake my head. He reaches over and takes my hand.

"I didn't want Shannon to think I play favorites because you're my wife. Boss man, huh? I like that. Can we role-play that tonight? You can play the submissive secretary. It'll be hot." He waggles his eyebrows.

"This isn't one of my books, Parker."

"You're right. It's better."

I laugh and he rubs a single tear lingering in the corner of my eye.

"Hey, you okay?"

"I got a call a little bit ago."

"From?"

"Wendy."

I give a weak smile and the tears start to well up again. I nod in confirmation, unable to choke out the words.

Parker's go soft.

Swallowing, I manage, "We're going to have a baby."

"A baby?" Parker chokes. He doesn't bother clearing his throat or trying to hide his tears.

"Yes."

A lump forms in my throat. I want to say something, yell, cheer, run around—do *something*. But, all I can manage is to sit with my husband. I fall into his arms, gripping his shirt.

"How in the world did I get so lucky?" he says.

"You know what?"

"Hmm?" He searches my happy, tear-streaked face and wipes away a tear as it slides down my cheek.

"I'm wondering the same thing." I'd follow this man anywhere if it meant being together forever.

My hair is sticking to the back of my neck so I twist it into a low side bun. The warm breeze makes its way into the house through the open kitchen windows, cooling me down a little. Birds' chirping punctuates the silence. It's the perfect evening to sit out on the deck with a glass of wine and unwind after our busy day.

It's been one week since we closed on our house.

I stand in our new kitchen, taking it all in, still amazed this house is ours. It's one of the biggest kitchens I've ever seen with top-of-the-line stainless steel appliances, a wet bar built into the center island, a six-burner stove, and a double oven. I can't cook, but this kitchen makes me want to have Genna give me a few lessons … or ten.

I trace the silver and white swirls in the shiny countertop that feels like glass. I feel weightless as I think of how Parker knew exactly what I'd want. I couldn't have picked a more perfect home for us.

In the living room, where Genna and Jean are finishing hanging pictures, my favorite sign is displayed next to the front door: He Stole Her Heart, She Stole His Last Name.

Under that is a photo that Genna took moments after Parker and I got engaged. I'm holding my left hand out, grinning up at Parker—who's giving me a loving smile. The sand is beautiful, the sky is ocean blue, and my hair is blowing wildly. I let myself drift to the memory of that day.

"Come on, Aundrea! Come play with us!" Parker yells. Parker and Jason had a veterinarian conference in West Palm Beach, about thirty minutes from his parents' place in Jupiter. Genna took it upon herself to declare a vacation.

I look up at his gorgeous smile. He's standing barefoot in the sand next to Jason with big aviator sunglasses on, and a smile that could melt any girl into a puddle. They've been playing Frisbee all morning while Genna and I tan. Actually, while we try to tan. We both tend to turn lobster red rather than golden brown.

"Nah! I'm good right here." I'm sitting in the white beach chair with my Kindle, a glass of cold white wine, and the hot sun beating down on my pale skin. I don't feel like moving.

I focus my attention back on my story, but a shadow falls over me, replacing the sunlight. I don't need to look up to know it's Parker.

"Hmm?" I ask, not looking up.

"Marry me."

That gets my attention. I look up, lowering my sunglasses to the tip of my nose to get a better look at him. When I see his smile, I laugh.

"Very funny."

"I'm not kidding," he says with a hint of amusement.

"Sure. Okay, and I don't like popcorn and pickle juice," I mock. Pushing my sunglass back on, I look back down at my Kindle. When the shadow doesn't move, I look back up. Parker's face has turned serious, his smile now a straight line.

I lose all feeling in my arms and legs. I can feel the blood rushing through my veins as the world around me mutes. My heart speeds up and all I can do is stare at Parker's face.

"You're serious?" I choke out.

Parker drops to both knees in the sand so his eyes are at my level. "As serious as I've ever been." I swallow hard, looking around. Genna has a big smile and Jason's sporting an equally enthusiastic grin.

"Pa — "

"Before you say anything, let me speak." He pauses, running a hand through his short blond locks. "Aundrea, I have never loved anyone the way that I love you." He takes his sunglasses off and his eyes are soft. I can see how nervous he is as he takes both my shaking hands into his. "Shit, this is a lot harder than I thought it would be." He laughs, looking around, then meets my eyes.

"The day you walked into my life is the day I knew I would never be the same. Here was this woman in the men's bathroom in the shortest, tightest, and hottest little black lace dress. I saw the shocked expression on your face and immediately fell in love with your big eyes. One look was all it took and I knew I was a goner. I swear, you saw right through me, and I knew I would stop at nothing to learn your name." He swallows before adding, "I needed to hear your voice, and it was as if you could read my mind because just then you spoke and, my God, your voice was so beautiful." His voice cracks at the last word, and he clears his throat.

Tears start to fall down my cheeks and I swallow around a lump in my throat.

Parker scoots closer to me. "Aundrea, you are mine in every way possible. Every time you walk into a room you make it brighter. You see the greatness in the world and in me. This past year and a half have been the best of my life, and it's all because of you. You complete me. I can't imagine going through my life without you by my side. Believe me when I say you would make me the happiest man on this planet if you agreed to be my wife."

"Parker."

My voice cracks. His name is all I can manage as my throat becomes tight. When I see him reach into his pocket and pull out a little green box, I gasp. I cover my mouth with both hands, looking from the box to his eyes.

"I've been carrying this with me since the day I bought it, waiting for the perfect moment and praying you wouldn't catch me with it." He looks down at the ring, then back at me, grinning. "I wanted to get you the biggest ring I could find, but when I saw this one, I knew it would be perfect for your delicate finger."

"It is perfect," I say, staring at it.

The ring is yellow gold with two rows of diamonds on either side of a large princess cut stone that sits much higher than the rest and is absolutely stunning.

"This isn't exactly where I thought I would ask you, but I can't think of a better moment. Marry me, please?"

I stare longingly at the ring in his hand with a million thoughts running through my head. He's asking the impossible from me. Something I swore I would never do. Marriage is forever. It's a commitment; an oath to stand by someone through the good and the bad.

Parker has seen me at my worst and my best. He's always by my side.

I want to stand by his.

Forever.

In truth, I never wanted to get married. I never thought I'd find love in the middle of battling cancer, either. But I did.

I want to marry Parker.

Taking a deep breath, I begin, "Parker, I never wanted to get married —"

"Before you break my heart and turn me down, let me just sa —"

"Shh…" I press my finger to his lips. "I never wanted to get married until I met you. You bring out a side of me that feels as if I can take on the world. I want to take on the world with you, Parker."

"You're saying yes?"

I nod.

"That's a yes?" he asks again, as if to convince himself.

"Yes!" I laugh.

Parker engulfs me into his arms, squeezing so tightly I have to tell him to let go so I can breathe. Laughing, we continue to look at one another.

"You're really going to marry me?"

"Yes, I'm going to marry you."

Kissing the top of my head, he keeps his arms securely around me. "I'm never letting you go, Aundrea."

"I won't let you."

"Earth to Aundrea." Jean waves her hand in front of my face.

"What? I'm sorry." My thoughts become fractured as I'm brought back.

"I said the guys are here with food. Are you ready to take a break?"

"Oh. Yeah, thanks."

I shake my head, my mind still foggy with the memory.

In the kitchen, I greet Kevin and Jason. Parker's taking out the plates that I just put away. Because everyone has been so gracious, offering to help us move in, we thought it would be nice to tell them our exciting news in person. Brandon and Amy had plans, so we made arrangements for them to come see the house soon.

Genna sets Hannah down, who's starting to get antsy. Parker walks over. "I got her; you go eat. What's wrong, baby girl?" he asks in a sweet voice.

Hannah starts cooing in his arms. "Oh, is that so?" She babbles some more and Parker continues talking to her as if they're having a conversation. His version of a baby voice is pretty adorable. Jean laughs at him, but I can only close my eyes and relish the sound of his voice.

"You're good with her," Genna says fondly.

When Parker makes Hannah giggle I open my eyes and watch. It's the perfect glimpse into what my future is about to become and I couldn't be happier.

"Have you talked to Wendy at all?" Jean asks.

I break into a wide grin, meeting Parker's eyes. My silence must give something away because when I look away from Parker, I see eight pairs of eyes on me.

I look among them, but before I can get a word out Genna bursts into tears. *Definitely overly emotional since having Hannah.*

"She's pregnant?" Jean probes.

Parker comes over to stand behind me, Hannah still in his arms.

I grin. "Yes."

Genna sobs and then lets out a high-pitched squeal that causes Hannah to giggle. "Dre! My baby sister is going to be a mommy! Does Mom know? When did you find out? How's Wendy doing? I can't believe you didn't say anything earlier!"

"Simmer down," I joke. "We just found out; we've spent the last few days processing it just the two of us. Wendy's doing really well. So far she's not feeling any different, but it's very early."

"And Mom and Dad?"

"You're the first to know."

Everyone chimes in their congratulations; then come the hugs.

"This is cause for celebration," Jean announces.

"To the bar!" Kevin cheers.

The rest of us laugh. Leave it to these two to find a reason to go out drinking.

"We're all for celebrating, but maybe on a night where I'm not on call," Parker teases.

"Friday?" Jason asks.

"We can get Mom and Dad to come down for the weekend to watch Hannah," Genna exclaims.

"I'm game," Parkers says, handing a happy Hannah to Jason.

"Me too." I smile.

"Oh, invite Amy," Genna says excitedly.

"I will."

Jean comes over and gives me another hug. "I couldn't be more excited and happy for you, Dre. You deserve every bit of happiness. I love you."

"I love you too."

When everyone leaves I send Amy a text asking if she's still up.

Amy: *Kind of. What's up?*

Me: *I'm sorry! Go back to sleep. I'll call you in the morning.*

My phone rings. "Hey, I'm sorry to wake you."

"You didn't." Her voice is sleepy. She tries to clear it but it doesn't help. "What's going on?"

"I wanted to call you earlier but it's been a crazy day." Silence. "Wendy's pregnant."

"Aundrea!" Her voice cracks, followed by a groggy cough. "That is incredible news."

"Parker and I are still shocked that this is real. I feel like I have to pinch myself just to make sure I'm not dreaming this life."

"That kind of news is definitely worth not being asleep for. Thank you for calling me."

"Always. I'll let you get back to sleep. First, though, if you're free Friday night we're going to go out and celebrate."

"I'll keep you posted. My dad wanted to take Ethan fishing this weekend, so that might work, actually."

"Will do; goodnight."

"Night. Oh, and Dre?"

"Yeah?"

"Don't worry about a thing. You got this." I don't reply and she doesn't wait for one before hanging up.

Back in the kitchen, Parker is finishing cleaning up. He wipes his hands after setting the last wine glass in the sink, then turns to me. He winks and I recognize the look in his eye. The look that says he's ready to ravish me right here and now.

"Can I help you?" I tease, scooting along the counter with a naughty grin.

"I got to thinking."

"Hmm?"

"We have to mark our territory."

I laugh, but he gives me a devious look. I know his looks all too well. I move quickly, but he snatches me. "Oh no you don't," I squeal.

He picks me up and puts me over his right shoulder. "Parker! Put me down!" I'm only half kidding. I try to kick, but he holds my legs down.

"The neighbors are going to hear you if you keep screaming," he says, amused.

"We don't have any neighbors." I giggle. All our neighbors are acres away, and we're separated by trees.

"Then you better scream really loud."

chapter THIRTEEN

Aundrea

I talk to Wendy every night this week, to check on her and to schedule her first OB appointment.

Jean drives back into town Friday night to go to Max's Bar with us—where Parker and I met. Genna suggested a few quiet restaurants we could go to but, in true Jean form, she wanted music, dancing, and drinks.

Amy and I texted over the last few days. She decided to stay at her parents' through the weekend but she insisted we get together this coming week to celebrate.

"Let's dance!" Jean screams into my ear. I nod, taking her hand. She leads the way, Genna holding my other hand as we squeeze through the crowd to the second level. Making our way front and center, we all start dancing foolishly and laughing at ourselves. The dance floor is packed and we're bumping elbows with those around us, but no one seems to mind. The music is blaring and I feel each pound of the bass deep within me.

It's a Shakira song screaming from the speakers and I move my hips with the beat. Because I haven't had much to drink, my dance moves are more reserved. I've never been a good dancer and am easily embarrassed by my awkward movements. Jean once described my dancing as uncontrolled seizing. *As opposed to controlled seizing?*

It doesn't take long before Parker joins me, pulling me hard against his chest. "I want to feel your hips move with mine," he growls into my ear. I can smell the beer on his breath as he moves in closer.

I oblige, pushing back into him, allowing his hands to hug my hips. We dance close for every song, paying no attention to whether it's fast or slow. My red halter top starts to stick to my back from the heat we're making. Parker doesn't seem to mind. In fact, he licks across my shoulder blade.

Parker eventually turns me to face him. I twine my arms around his neck and he rests his hands on my hips. We sway together, making eye contact. "Do you know what I'm thinking about right now?" he asks, brushing his mouth against mine.

"No, what?"

"Our first night. How we met and danced right here. How hard you made me every time you pressed your ass against me. I wanted to take you then and there, and then again in front of the bathroom later that night."

"You should have."

"Really?" He lifts an eyebrow. "You sure about that?" *No. Maybe.*

"That night I didn't care." *That's the truth.* "All I could think about was you taking me. I even told myself I didn't care who was around us; I'd let you."

He groans, pulling me close enough to feel his hardness. Just feeling him excites me. "What about now?"

"What about it?" I make my words sound playful, secretly hoping he's going to suggest something that will take care of the ache that's starting to form between my thighs.

"What if I said I wanted to take you right now?" *Thank you, sweet little baby Jesus!*

"I'd say, take me."

Parker breaks our hold at lightning speed. Before I can even exhale or comprehend what exactly is going on, he's pulling me down the steps and toward the bathrooms. Giving each door a quick look, he opens the women's first.

"Excuse me," he says apologetically to the woman washing her hands. She looks confused and I give her a remorseful smile. Letting the door close behind him, he pulls me to the men's room. I'm excited just at the memory of our first encounter.

After making sure no one is inside, Parker quickly pulls me in after him. He locks the door the second it slams shut. One hand on mine and the other around my waist, he turns me around and presses against me, then pushes us backward until I hit the counter.

"Are you serious?"

He cups my cheek and leans in, whispering, "I'm going to make you feel so good."

He's serious.

I whimper at his words. He knows my body inside and out; knows exactly what it needs. And right now it needs him.

Turning me around so I'm looking in the mirror, he slips his hand inside my shirt, lightly tracing my skin. He pushes my bra aside and tugs on my nipple, which hardens under his touch as my eyes flutter closed.

"Open your eyes. I want you to watch me."

This all seems too intimate for a public bathroom, but I oblige.

The look on his face in the mirror shows that he's hungry for me.

He holds my hip and rolls my nipple in small circles. He flexes his hips, pushing himself into my backside so I can feel how hard he is. Pulling me firmly against him, he drops light kisses along my neck and I tilt my head to the side, giving him full access. He kisses my ear, then leisurely licks at my skin, tasting every inch of me he can reach.

"You always smell so good. Like fucking pears and honey. I can never get enough of your scent, Aundrea."

My head falls back onto his shoulder when he cups my

breasts firmly, then begins to rub my breasts, massaging them roughly while rocking his hips into me.

"Look in the mirror. I want you to watch yourself as I play with you."

The passion and foreplay at the beginning of any sexual encounter with Parker is always exciting.

I crave this part, right here. The way I tingle with each touch. The way I ache and throb for him. The electricity that pulls me to him.

"Parker," I breathe.

"Don't worry, babe. I got you."

His hands move from my breasts and I moan at the loss. I don't have to wait long before they're back, running up my thighs and under my skirt. He holds one thigh while he trails a hand to my wet center.

"I love that you're ready for me," he groans.

He slips a finger inside the cotton and taunts me, tracing along the outer edges of my slick folds. I quiver from his touch, begging him for more as my knees shake.

Parker wraps his arm around my waist, pulling me even closer. "Do you feel how wet you are? How much you're craving me, want me inside of you? I can almost feel your tightness wrapped around me and hear the sounds you'll make."

"Parker, please," I urge.

His finger slips inside me, and my eyes roll back in my head at the sudden entrance. "Watch me. Watch the way I make you feel good. The way your lips part and your skin heats with my touch. Watch me, Aundrea."

I open my eyes and he slips another finger inside. "God, you feel so fucking good," he murmurs, moving his fingers faster and deeper. Then he glides up to my swollen clit, rubbing me in hard, fast circles that have me rocking against his palm.

"Right there, don't move … oh my God."

"Not yet, babe, I want to feel you around me when you explode." He stops touching me and I wince at the unexpected loss. Parker laughs. "Don't worry, babe."

He turns me around and lifts me onto the counter. I pull my skirt up to my waist and Parker pulls down my yellow thong and drops it on the counter next to me.

I unbutton his pants quickly and he pulls out the hardness that I so desperately need.

I spread my legs, opening myself to him. I've never had sex in a public bathroom before and, honestly, I find it exciting. Adrenaline washes through me at the thought that we could be caught, which just excites me even more.

"Not so fast." He pauses, staring at me.

"What?" I ask in frustration.

He looks down and I follow his gaze. He's stroking himself slowly. I watch as he plays with himself, wrapping his hand tighter around his shaft.

"You do this to me. You make me hard with just one look — the look that burns in your eyes when you're thinking about me being inside you. You drive me crazy … I want to make you just as crazy."

"By provoking me?"

"No, by not being allowed to touch me. Hold onto the edge of the counter and don't let go."

"Parker," I groan. I'm not about to just sit there while he has sex with me.

"Do it," he says sternly, still stroking himself. "Or you get to sit there and watch me finish myself off."

"Parker!" *Is this man crazy?*

He winks. Reluctantly, I give in and hold onto the counter.

"Good. Now, don't let go, or I stop." He pulls me closer to the edge of the counter and traces my folds with his finger. I close my eyes and wait for him to enter me, but he doesn't. When he lets out a small sigh of pleasure, I open my eyes again.

He's sucking his finger, sampling me. "You taste so. Fucking. Good."

"Pa—"

He thrusts inside of me without warning.

"Shit!" I scream. It's so loud I know whoever is outside the bathroom heard it. Parker moves inside me, deep and fast, filling every inch. He slams harder into me with each thrust and I start to call out his name.

"Shh, babe." His hand comes up to cover my cries of pleasure.

I try to keep my moaning to a minimum, but he makes it difficult as he pushes me closer and closer to the edge. My head falls back, my lips part, and I hold onto the counter with everything I have.

Parker kisses my neck. "Come on, baby, let me feel you."

I call out his name as I release the high within me. I shudder with waves of pleasure as Parker slows down his pace. We kiss, our tongues finding one another. He tastes of beer with a hint of me. When he finds his own release, my mouth muffles the sound of him calling out my name.

"Wow."

"Yeah, wow," Parker says, breathing heavily.

"I've always wanted to do that," I say, releasing the counter and wrapping my arms around his neck.

"What's that?"

"Have sex in a bathroom."

"Really?"

I wave it off as if it's no big deal. I never thought it would actually ever happen.

"Huh, I never would have guessed that."

"What can I say? You've awakened my senses and made me want to explore everything in life. Now, handsome, let's get cleaned up and back out to our table before the search party comes after us."

We give each other a quick once over and exit the bathroom. When we round the corner, Jason, Genna, Kevin, and Jean are all smiles as the waitress drops off another round of drinks.

"Did you two get lost?" Jean taunts.

"Or fall in?" Genna counters.

Parker and I look at each other, shaking our heads. "We

ran into a classmate of mine," I explain quickly.

"Whatever. Look at their faces. Those two totally just fucked," Kevin says.

"What? No we didn't." I shake my head, then sit and chug the water in front of me. The cold liquid is cool and refreshing after our recent heat.

"Right, that's why Parker's zipper is down and your shirt is flipped up at the bottom. Looks like a quickie to me."

Parker and I both quickly look down at ourselves, then each other, but we're both dressed correctly.

"Gotcha!" He breaks out in laughter. "You two are *so* busted."

I shake my head, but don't hide my smile. Parker sips his beer with a faint smile while the others stare at us.

"Do you blame me? Look at her?" Parker finally says against the rim of his beer.

I flush. Parker reaches over and traces the color I know is in my cheeks.

"Well, then. Now that we've established those two just got lucky, how about we drink!" Jean chants, raising her martini glass.

"I'll toast to that!" Kevin says.

Parker leans back in his chair and gives me a wink as he sips his beer. I wink back, tasting my pineapple lemon drop martini.

We spend the rest of our night tossing back drinks, dancing, and reminiscing about the last three years. It's times like this that make me grateful I'm surrounded by such amazing people.

☙ ❧

Rain spatters me as I run into Mayo Clinic the following week.

The security guard holds the door open when he sees me coming, giving me his usual tight nod.

"Thank you," I say as I rush past him.

There is a crowd by the elevators so I decide to take the stairs, my wet sneakers squeaking with each step. On the third floor, I walk into the oncology office, pushing my wet hair out of my face.

When I get to the back, though, Amy isn't here yet. Casey walks in and freezes when she sees me.

"Hey! I thought Amy was coming in today? I haven't seen her in weeks." I've been looking forward to this day. We made plans to go out for lunch and talk nothing but baby.

Casey's face falls and her shoulders hunch.

"What is it?" I'm wary.

I can see the pain in her wide, bloodshot eyes. "Dre." She sounds afraid to say anything else.

"What happened?" I can't take a step closer.

Her chin starts to quaver and she bites her bottom lip.

A light prickling sensation hits the back of my neck. The kind that tells me something is horribly wrong.

Her mouth open and closes. An uneasy feeling takes over—that sickening feeling that sets in the pit of my stomach—and I can't take it. I know something's wrong and I need Casey to spit it out. It feels like there's a hundred-pound weight on my sternum.

"What is it?"

Casey looks over my shoulder instead of at me. She opens her mouth again to speak but no words come out, only the agonizing, horrifying sound of her cries.

Watching her, listening to her, it's as if all of her pain passes right into me.

My shoulders begin to quake. I don't know exactly what's going on but I know it has to be completely terrible for Casey to be crying the way she is. Her make-up runs down her face as she hurriedly digs for a tissue.

"I-I I'm so s-orry, Dre."

I take a slow step toward her, holding my hands in front of me so I don't startle her. "Take a deep breath, Casey." She tries, but her sobs are uncontrollable. "Sit down." I pull out a chair and ease her feather-light body into it. "Deep breaths."

She drops her head between her knees and I direct her breathing. I take a few of my own deep breaths. When she finally controls herself I look around for someone. *Where is everyone?*

"What happened?"

Her head snaps up, mouth wide and face smeared with snot and mascara-tinged tears. She looks around, closing her eyes tightly. I brace myself.

"Amy."

My throat feels like I've swallowed a handful of needles. "What about Amy?"

"She passed away last night."

chapter

FOURTEEN

Aundrea

I didn't brace myself enough, apparently, because I fall hard against the cold floor.

I feel like I've fallen into a black hole: no light, no hope. In astrophysics, we call that boundary the event horizon. Nothing from the other side can reach you there and you continue speeding up as the gravity waves pull you to the center.

I'm cold and numb. Casey's speaking too fast for me to follow. I can't make out a single word. I just sit, unmoving, staring into space from my black hole.

"What do you mean? She was doing okay. She was okay!" My voice is shaky, almost unrecognizable. "I just talked to her last week. We were getting together today!" My voice rises with each word.

A few employees come walking around the corner to see what's going on. When I look their way, they won't meet my eyes. Everyone here knows how close Amy and I are. *Were.*

"Dre, Amy stopped full treatment last year."

"Stopped treatment?" I shake my head. Everything feels fuzzy. "That's not possible. I know her. I know her! She finished treatment when we met. She is a survivor. We are survivors!"

"Her cancer metastasized to her bones, Aundrea. There wasn't anything further that could be done. I'm so sorry."

"But I saw her. She was doing well."

"She was on maintenance chemo to help keep her stable, but it spread so fast over the last two months. Nothing was working and over the last month it took over. She only allowed you to see what she wanted."

I don't understand why she didn't tell me. Why she led me to believe everything was okay.

If Casey's still talking to me I don't hear a thing. Everything inside of me is gone. Whatever life or soul that was inside of me has left my body.

I stand, pushing past her and force myself to keep walking. It finally hits me when I take my first step down the stairs. Everything comes crashing down when my foot hits the cement in the stairwell. It sounds like a crack of thunder.

Pushing myself, I run down the stairs, holding onto the railing to keep myself from falling. It's the only thing holding me up.

The security guard jumps up when he sees me. "Are you okay?"

I wave him off and fling the door open. The rain slashes at my face and the pain feels good. I stand and let it pierce my skin. My heart is shattering into a million shards, as if it were made of glass.

I clutch my chest, falling to my knees on the sidewalk in front of the clinic. I can't even be certain if I'm still breathing. People walk past me; a few stop, but they sound distant. I clutch my chest, begging the burning pain to stop. She's gone. Casey's words run through my head over and over again, cutting deeper each time. *She passed away last night.*

"Ma'am? Are you okay?"

"Do you need help?"

"Is someone with you?"

"Does she need an ambulance?"

Ignoring them all, I get to my feet and run to my car. The

blood orange sun looks like fire in the sky.

I don't know where I'm going when I get into my car, but I peel out of the lot as fast as I can. I try calling Parker's cell. I need him.

He doesn't answer.

I try again. *Nothing.*

I don't bother calling the clinic. I know he has a full schedule and the thought of driving to the clinic makes me sick. I can't be there right now. I'm in no shape for that.

But I don't want to go home and be alone.

I try Parker's direct line, but when there's no answer I drive to Genna's on instinct.

I'll keep trying him, but right now I need to focus on the road. The rain comes down harder as I speed up.

I'm not really sure how I get to Genna's, but I zone back in as I'm pulling into her driveway next to my parents' car. I forgot they were still here.

The pain won't stop. The ache in my heart grows stronger as I shut the car off and sit with nothing but the sounds of rain and wind crashing against the windshield. I slump forward over the steering wheel and cry into my hands. My shoulders shake so hard they start to ache.

Suddenly, I'm furious. I hit the steering wheel. "Why!" I scream at the top of my lungs. "Why would you take her away? Why?" Pain slices through me, but it doesn't release any of my agony. It just stays, burning and aching.

I need this feeling to go away. I'm so mad that Amy didn't tell me what was happening and hurt that she didn't trust me. Didn't she think I could handle the news? As my tears continue to fall, I think back to the last few months and how blind I was to it all. The longing looks she gave Ethan, the date nights with Brandon, the lab draws, spending more time with her family, and all this talk about life and embracing fear.

Opening my car door, I run to the house. I'm not sure what I need or who I need at this point. But I know I need to be inside. I need to scream at something — or someone. I need to make the hurt go away.

Laughter comes from the house the second I open the door, but it stops abruptly when I slam the door.

"Hello?" Genna cautiously asks from somewhere inside.

My mom comes to the top of the stairs and sees me. "Dre? Are you okay?"

"No," I manage to get out, but my voice doesn't sound like me.

She rushes down the stairs.

"What is it? What happened?"

Genna runs over too.

"Make it stop, please make it stop."

"What, honey?" my mom asks, rubbing my back.

"The pain."

"Dre, you're scaring me. What happened?" Genna asks.

"Amy." It hurts to even say her name. Knowing she's no longer here and that this isn't some terrible nightmare.

"Your friend?" my mom asks, while Genna says, "What happened?"

I nod. "She passed away last night."

One of them gasps.

"It's okay, Dre. Deep breaths." Genna's voice is soothing. She rubs small, tender circles on my back.

"I can't. I can't breathe." The pain is only increasing.

"Honey, I know this is difficult. But you need to breathe."

"I can't!"

"Mom, give her a minute," Genna instructs. "She just learned her friend died."

"I understand that, but I need her to calm down."

They're talking about me as if I'm not even here.

I cry out as the pain intensifies. "My chest."

"Sweetie, take deep breaths."

"I can't … the pain. Oh my God. Make it stop! I can't make it stop!"

"I need you to calm down so something doesn't to happen to *you*!"

"What?" I croak.

I start to panic, so I put my hands on my knees and bend over, trying to get a breath. But it doesn't come.

Am I going to end up like Amy? Holy hell. This is a fucking nightmare.

Fear. It's all around us. It finds a way inside, lodging deep within, refusing to surrender. It latches on, following you on this path called life. The way it makes our bodies tremble through our core, perspire with one thought, or makes our hearts feel as if they're coming to a standstill, causing all blood flow to rush from our head to our toes. It's the one word that can instantly cause our breathing to become slow and labored, stirring up the worst emotions within.

Suddenly my chest becomes too tight to bear. My legs go numb and my arms feel weak. My heart is beating too fast and, no matter how much I pray for it to slow, and the tight pain to go away, it doesn't.

I'm gasping for air. "My chest. It's too tight." I claw at my shirt, as if I could rip it off. The once soft fabric now feels like fire, burning away my flesh.

"Mom, I don't think she's okay!"

"Aundrea?!"

"I can't breathe. My ... tight ... the pain ... it won't stop. I can't feel my arms, or ..." Oh my God, this is it.

I fall to my knees.

"Is she having a heart attack?" Panicky, Genna stands and yells for my dad.

Every dream I've had, every sense of hope—everything I've feared is burning them away right before my eyes.

Death.

It's easy to forget what matters most when you're distracted by your deepest fear, which, in my case, is leaving behind everyone I cherish most. Sometimes it's the most disturbing thoughts that tunnel their way to your core and hold on, no matter how hard you try to shake them.

The afterlife doesn't scare me. The unknown can be magical when you really think about it. The beauty of possibility.

There are muffled voices around me, yelling and screaming, but my eyes are frozen. I can't move my head to see who's speaking. I can't even be certain where I am at the moment.

I begin to feel like I'm floating and it's then that I realize I'm being put on a stretcher. There are two men yelling. *Why are they yelling? Are they yelling at me?*

A cold rush of air startles me as a mask is put over my face. It's the first time I get a deep, fulfilling breath since this all started.

"You're going to be okay. Keep your eyes open for me, okay?" one of the men instructs, leaning close to my face.

I try to nod, but he shakes his head. "Don't try to move." I go cold, every limb gone numb. Then, pain.

I don't think I've ever felt so much pain in all my life. It's as if a hundred men are standing on top of me, stabbing my chest with razor-sharp knives. I swear, with each jab of pain I can hear the crack of the blades stabbing deeper inside of me, slowly ripping me apart. Then the pain pierces my heart and I cry out.

"Someone needs to call Parker!" Genna screams.

The men start running and I feel like I'm flying. The wind washes over me and it's almost calming.

My surroundings go blurry as I'm lifted. Everything is happening so fast. My shirt is ripped open and freezing stickers are placed on my chest.

Cries fill my ears, drowning out the loud banging from the men moving around. I don't know where I am, but when I hear my mom say, "Parker, its Aundrea. We're going to the hospital," I let my eyes drift closed and just pray the pain will stop. And that Parker will get to me before it's too late.

chapter FIFTEEN

Parker

"Well, Coco is looking good. I won't need to see her back for another six months." I give the black lab a small pat, then smile at its owner, Beth.

"Thanks, Dr. Jackson."

There's a loud knock on the exam door.

I open it to see a worried Shannon.

"Is everything okay?" I ask.

She pauses before speaking. "The phones are crazy this morning with Aundrea not here, so a few calls have gone to the answering machine. I just checked the messages and there were two, one from Aundrea's mom and another from Genna."

I push back the uneasy feeling. "And what did they say?"

"Donna's said to check your voicemail. Genna's message was screaming and very difficult to understand. She sounded scared."

I push past her and run to my office. Shannon yells after me, "I was able to make out that you need to get to the hospital right now!"

I dash around the corner, grab my keys and cell phone, and run to my car.

"Parker!" Jason yells after me. "Genna called me. They're taking Aundrea to the hospital. She thinks she's having a heart attack."

I don't even stop to reply, just run as fast as I can to my car.

At the car, all the blood rushes out of my head and I'm so dizzy I almost fall forward. My tires squeal as I pull out, that I'm pretty certain I've burned rubber marks into the tar. *Please let her be okay.*

When I'm on the main road, I listen to the voicemail from Donna. It's only then that I see all my missed calls. *Fuck, Aundrea tried to call me! I wasn't there for her.*

Donna says, "Parker, its Aundrea. We're going to the hospital. It's her heart." Her words are so frantic and her voice so worried that I drop the phone. I don't wait to hear to the rest. I press down hard on the gas, but I'm still not going fast enough.

I need to get to her.

To be with her.

I need to make sure she's okay.

Her face comes into view, fracturing my thoughts. The smile she gave me this morning. Fuck, I love her smile. Picturing her smiling face makes me think of our wedding day. How happy she was.

How happy *we* were.

I close my eyes, forcing myself to breathe slowly and deeply. When I open them, all I see is her. My breath catches in the back of my throat. Before me is the woman who has changed me.

I exhale.

She flashes me the biggest smile I've ever seen and all I can do is smile back. I can see the spark in her eyes even from this distance, and I swear everything around me just stopped. It's like she's walking in slow motion, with eyes only for me. She's clutching her bouquet so tight her knuckles are white. She's in the most beautiful pastel pink gown, and it makes her look like a queen. I can't believe this woman is mine.

I give her a wink and she blows me a kiss. When I give her another smile, her whole face brightens. It makes my heart flip. She can bring me to my knees with that one look. The look that says she can't imagine being with anyone else; she's beyond in love with me; she was meant for me.

It's the look of someone who is hopelessly in love.

There is no one else in the room. It's only her and me, with our eyes locked on one another. I can feel the pull we have on each other us, drawing her closer to me like a magnet. Aundrea has awakened my soul. She's the woman that I will spend the rest of my life with. The woman I will love indefinitely.

When she reaches me, Jay gives Aundrea a quick kiss on the cheek and releases her with a short sob. I shake his hand before I take hers, both of us still grinning.

"Hi," I whisper.

"Hey there, handsome," she whispers back.

She squeezes my hand, the light pinch letting me know that I'm not dreaming. That she's here. That we're here and we're becoming one.

I don't even notice the pastor has begun the ceremony until she says my name a couple of times. "Parker, are you ready for your vows?"

"Yes, yes, I am," I say, dazed.

We decided to write our own vows. There are no words but our own – and I'm still not sure they're enough – to describe the love we share.

I watch Aundrea's chest rise and fall slowly. She flushes and her eyes fill with tears before I even open my mouth.

I don't release her hands, as I begin. "Aundrea, today I stand before you to make a promise. A promise to make you smile every day, to stand beside you and make memories with you, to love you, protect you, respect and support you, and honor you. You inspire me to be a better man and to be stronger. Your love is the reason I exist, and I will cherish it with all of my being and for all infinity, as time doesn't end with us."

Aundrea wipes at her tears, getting herself under control. I brush a few away with my thumb.

She clears her throat and swallows down the last of her tears before speaking. *"You never backed down when it came to us. You fought for us, for our love and a life together. You are my love, my life, and my friend. You are my home. I make a promise to live for you, make a lifetime of dreams with you, and, more than anything, I promise to love you from here through eternity, for death will not separate us."*

No "until death do us part" for us.

When we're announced Mr. and Mrs. Parker Jackson, Aundrea flashes me the same smile she did when she took her first step toward me down the aisle. I've waited to hear those words since I asked her to marry me and don't wait even a second to kiss her. I scoop her into my arms and bring my mouth down on hers. Our lips move effortlessly, uniting us as one.

Forever.

This is the woman I will move heaven and earth for. I believe everyone is destined for one soul. My soul was destined to meet Aundrea's. Our love was made for each other.

Pulling into the hospital parking lot, the realization of where I am comes back to me. I throw my door open and run through the emergency doors. I don't even know if I parked in an actual parking spot, but I couldn't care less at this point. I don't even bother closing my door or shutting the car off.

The only thing that matters is getting to my wife.

When I see the emergency lobby I run to the desk.

"My wife, Aundrea Jackson. She was brought here."

"Ok, sir, keep calm and I'll look."

Keep calm?! I scan the waiting room for Donna, Jay, or Genna, but don't see anyone.

"Please! Can you hurry up! She was brought here a while ago. I need to see her! I need to be with her!" I yell at the poor woman and she presses buttons faster.

"I'm checking, sir, please calm down. I don't want to call security."

"Call them!" I threaten.

I know she's doing her best, but I don't know what's

going on and every second counts. "Please," I urge.

"What did you say her name was?"

"Aundrea Jackson. March fourteenth—"

"Parker?"

I turn around to see Donna standing there.

"Donna!" I rush to her. "Where is she? What's going on?" She doesn't speak. "Donna!"

She flinches. "I don't know." She barely gets the words out. "They won't tell us anything."

I fall back and Jay comes out of nowhere, catching me.

"What happened?"

Donna pulls herself together. I can see the pain in her face, but she forces her words out. "She came home from Mayo after learning … hearing about …"

"Spit it out!" I'm not trying to be a prick, but need to know what's going on with my wife. "What happened?"

Genna speaks up. "Amy died and Aundrea came over, hysterical. I think she had a heart attack?"

"What?" This can't be happening. This isn't real.

Jay steps forward. "The doctor on call paged Dr. James to come in. That's all we know right now. They did an EKG in the ambulance, but wouldn't tell me anything, no matter how much I pressed. As soon as we got here they whisked her away."

Donna breaks into tears and Jay goes to comfort her. His own eyes are swollen.

"Nurse!" I yell, going back to the desk. "I need to speak with the doctor immediately."

"Sir, if you take a seat I'll let him know you'd like to speak with him."

"What is it with this place? I don't have any idea what's going on with my wife—if she's okay, or even where she is! I need some answers!"

"Excuse me, sir." It's a security guard.

Before I can speak a loud announcement comes over the intercom, "Code blue, ER room 3312. Code blue, ER room 3312. Anesthesia is needed to room 3312." The loud voice repeats the code again and I turn around, looking for a door. A door to get me to the exam rooms.

When I see one, I run over to it, bypassing the security guard.

As I run, I look for room numbers, scanning them as fast as I can. A crew dressed in blue scrubs run past me and I follow.

I don't have time to think or react. What I need is to be with her. I push all negative thoughts aside.

Voices yell behind me, trying to get me to stop, but I ignore them. Finding the room the staff went into it, I stop. I can't see anything but nurses and doctors surrounding the bed.

"Push it to 300!"

"Clear!"

"Nothing. Push it to 350!"

The body in the bed jerks, and I brace myself in the doorframe, knuckles turning white from my grip. Everything around me stops. My vision is a blur.

My own breathing is labored.

I've watched her die one too many times already. I won't allow that to happen now. I won't watch her die!

"Sir! You can't be here," a nurse says, rushing toward me.

"No! Please! Please, she needs me! I need to be with her!" My voice cracks and I stop myself, realizing my words are from one of my own nightmares.

Oh. My. God.

This cannot be happening. I can't be losing her. No! This is not how it's supposed to be. We're supposed to grow old together. Live a life together! And have this baby.

I drop to my knees.

The pain slices through me and I scream.

I feel numb for a second, then the pain cuts deep inside of me, throbbing with each word the nursing staff calls out.

"Parker?" My eyes fly open.

I whip around. Aundrea is standing behind me, next to two security guards. She's in a white robe, clutching the fabric at her side with one hand while holding onto her IV pole with the other. Tubes are attached to her hand and snake underneath her gown.

Her face is blank and pale. She looks weak, but she's still her.

"Aundrea?" My voice cracks. I blink a few times. *Is this real?* I look away from her and to the body on the bed before me. I don't know who that is, but it's not my wife.

I rush to her, tripping in the process. I land at her feet, clutching her legs and pulling her down to me.

The two men are saying something to me, but I don't even hear.

"You're okay?" I scan her up and down, searching for something to be wrong, but I don't see it. She's right in front of me. Alive.

"You're alive." A feeling of relief washes over me, followed by a wave of nausea. I think I'm going to be sick. "I thought—my God, Aundrea, I thought that was you."

"Shh," she says, pulling me to her.

I latch onto her robe, pulling her close so I can kiss her head, cheeks, eyes, nose, and mouth. I kiss every inch of her that I can reach.

"Aundrea, I need you back in your room. Now," Dr. James says sternly from behind us.

"Sir, you can't be back here!" the security guard yells.

"It's okay. This is the patient's husband," Dr. James replies.

The men give me a stern look before turning away in a huff.

I wrap my arm around Aundrea, helping her back to her room and into bed.

Dr. James follows.

"What happened? Are you okay? They said they thought you were having a heart attack. My God, Aundrea, I was so worried." I study her as I help her into bed.

"I don't know."

Turning to look at Dr. James, Aundrea's hand in mine,

I say, "Everything has been going well. I don't … I don't understand. What happened?"

"Everything *is* going well. It wasn't her heart." Dr. James says.

We both look at him. "What's going on Dr. James?"

He addresses Aundrea. "Your EKG came back clear. The other tests were also negative. What you experienced was a panic attack. It's common to get these mixed up because the symptoms are very similar to a heart attack. However, your family did the right thing by calling an ambulance. Especially given your state and your health."

"She had a panic attack?" I confirm.

He nods. "Aundrea, I want to see you in my office in a week for a check-up. In the meantime, take it easy and rest. We're going to hold you for the night, just as a precaution. You need to understand you're at greater risk of having a heart attack due to your cardiomyopathy. Getting your heart worked up, like today, can send it into overdrive. It tries to catch up, pumping twice as fast, and that's not good. Stress is not good for you. You need to find a way to keep yourself under control."

Aundrea hangs on his words, nodding. A few tears slide down her cheeks.

"I'm going to change the dosage of your medication slightly, and give you a prescription for Ativan to help with the anxiety you're having."

I thank Dr. James and assure him we'll schedule an appointment with him for next week.

When he leaves, I look down at my beautiful wife. The woman who means the most to me in the entire world.

"Aundrea?" She doesn't answer me, so I say it again. I need to hear her voice. She needs to talk to me.

"Amy pa … Amy … She's g-go-" She drops her head into her hands and cries.

I pull her into my side, holding her as tightly as I can. I rock us back and forth.

"I heard. Shh, it's going to be okay. I promise, everything

will be okay."

"No. No! This is not okay." She pushes out of my arms. "I hate the word okay at times like these! It's clearly *not* okay!"

"Aundrea?" I reach for her, but she scoots out of my grasp. Moving around the cords connected to her, she moves to the other side of the bed. She holds her hands up to keep me away.

"This is exactly what I didn't want to happen."

I look at her, confused.

My face falls. My sadness from moments ago is replaced with hurt. "What are you talking about?"

I don't move any closer, giving her the space she needs.

"This!" she screams, holding her arms out. "It's like everything came crashing down. My fear. She's gone and I have this stupid heart condition and … and that could be me one day! You knew that was a fear of mine and yet …"

"Yet what?" My voice sounds as angry as I feel.

"You still pressed the idea of having a family."

"Wait just one minute." I step around the foot of the bed and over to her.

"Why did I let you talk me into this?" Her voice sounds broken. I can hear the pain behind her words, but I ask anyway.

"Into what?"

"This life. You knew I was afraid. You knew it scared me. I wasn't the marrying type, but you still asked!"

"Hold on!" I step closer to her and she backs away into the corner of the wall.

"No. This is exactly what I was afraid of."

I'm so confused. Hurt even. I don't understand why she's doing this.

"Amy! She's gone, and look who is left behind to feel the pain. Ethan and Brandon. Her family, friends … me! You don't know what it's like to watch your nightmare come to life! I told you my biggest fear was leaving my loved ones behind. What happened with Amy, Brandon, and Ethan? That could be us, Parker. I don't want that."

"I don't know!?" I yell and she flinches. We've never fought in all our years together. Had disagreements? Of course. But we've never raised our voices to one another.

In a flash I'm standing nose to nose with her. "I've watched you die in my dreams and I just watched that nightmare be played out in front of me. You wanted this just as much as I did. Don't you for one second point that finger at me. Fuck, Aundrea. I'm so incredibly and deeply sorry about Amy, and my heart aches for her and her family, but don't put this all on me. I get that you're hurt and want to yell at someone, but don't blame me for the life *we* both want."

She slides to the floor, crying. She pulls at her hair then covers her face. "Fuck cancer. I hate what it's done to me. I hate what it's done to my friend, and I hate what it's taken away from her."

I pull her into my lap. She grabs onto my shirt, clawing at my chest to bring us even closer. She cries hard into my chest, her tears wetting my shirt.

Watching her go through this is unbearable. I know she doesn't mean what she said. I know she's hurting and needs to let out her frustration, so I give her what she needs.

I comfort her.

"I'll never hear her voice again. I'll never hear her laugh, or see her smile."

"I know, babe. I know. It's going to be okay. I got you."

"Make it stop, Parker. Please make it stop. I don't want to feel it anymore, please."

My shoulders shake as I begin to cry with her. "I want to, babe. Lord knows I want to."

"I saw what my life would be like if my cancer came back, or if I had a heart attack."

I hold onto her shoulders and look her in the eyes. "No. You did *not* get a glimpse into your future. You want a glimpse? We'll drive to St. Paul right now and you can stare long and hard at the woman who is growing our baby. *That* is your future, Aundrea. Not this. You are going to grow old with me and we're going to watch our children grow up *together.*

"I don't understand why people are taken away from us before they're ready. But when the path of your life changes, you have to let it. You have to embrace it, Aundrea. I'm not saying it's easy, but I promise you, everything works out in the end."

"Sometimes the strong ones need to lean on someone, too. You can't always be the one to make everything perfect, Dre," Aundrea whispers to herself as if she's repeating something someone else told her. I give her time to reassure herself that it's okay to lean on someone.

Me, I hope.

We sit together and let the tears fall.

We cry for Amy. For the life she'll never have.

We cry for Brandon. For the wife he'll never get to hold again.

We cry for Ethan. For growing up without his mother.

I cry for the woman in my arms and all the pain she's had to endure.

I cry for the woman I thought I lost.

chapter

SIXTEEN

Aundrea

I don't move.

I can't.

I've been putting off this day, refusing to let reality sink in. Parker's been coming in and out of our bedroom for the last hour trying to get me out of bed. The funeral is in an hour, but I can't bring myself to get up. I've watched people die around me. It's hard not to when you get treatment in a room full of people. Some come out on top while others … aren't so lucky. But I've never lost someone so unexpectedly. Let alone someone so close to me.

There's a light knock on the door.

"Aundrea?" Jean's voice is quiet. "You ready?"

I turn so I'm facing her and open one eye. She's wearing a knee-length black dress. Very simple and classic. Very Jean.

"Is anyone ever ready to bury their friend?"

Closing my eye, I let the darkness in, but it can't quite drown out the sound of footsteps. When the bed dips, I turn onto my back and stare at the ceiling. I try to count the swirls in the texture of our white ceiling, but soon lose count. Jean doesn't say a word.

I know what she's doing. She's waiting for me to open

up. To let it out, whatever it is.

I count to ten, then twenty, waiting for the words to form. But they don't. Tears start when I reach fifty, and when I hit eighty they still haven't stopped.

Jean takes my hand and lies on her side, facing me. It takes me a few moments, but eventually I turn onto my side. I keep counting as the tears fall. When Jean starts to cry, I close my eyes. I can't stand the pain in her eyes. Once I reach one hundred, the words come.

"Are you afraid to die?" My voice is scratchy.

"No," she whispers, wiping her tears.

"Me either."

"I know."

"I'm not ready to say goodbye."

"Death never gets easier."

I take a deep breath before letting everything inside of me out. Jean somehow always gets me to open up, even if I don't make any sense when I do.

"It's not fair that people have to die before we get it. Amy has talked me through so much these last couple months, and helped me see the beauty in everything. She's really made me want overcome the fear that's been holding me back. But, it's her death that's finally made me open my eyes. I've spent the last three days in a haze, thinking about everything she's left behind, and that's not the life I want. It's not fair that she had to die to really make me see the ramifications of it all. To make me realize that I haven't been living my life to its full potential these last few months. Like, really *living*. I've been working toward the perfect future, but lately I've only looked at the future as if I weren't in it. I want to be in it, Jean."

"Then live, Dre. Living was your struggle then. It's not your struggle now. You've always looked at the positives, never letting death knock you down. That's never been you, so don't let it start being you now. You're one of the most courageous women I've ever known."

"Where's my courage now?" I feel like a coward hiding

out in my bed.

Jean jabs me in the chest. "Right here. It hasn't left you. You're grieving, and that's okay. But, it's also okay to let it out. You don't need to hide."

I know she's right. Even the strongest of us have weaknesses and moments that make us feel small. But I guess you can't really overcome weakness or fear until you're faced with them.

I close my eyes for a moment, then I take a deep breath. "I'm ready."

⁓ℭ ℭ⁓

I fidget with my thumb ring and tap my feet as we get near the church. Parker doesn't say anything. No one does.

Jean and Kevin sit in silence in the back seat and Parker focuses on the road.

When we pull into the parking lot, Parker opens my door. He takes my hand, giving me the support I need.

Everyone's in black except me. Amy hated black, so the last thing I wanted to do was wear it to her funeral. Instead, I chose blue—her favorite color.

We find seats in the back pew. I can't fathom sitting up close, being next to the casket. I watch as people walk up and pay their respects to Amy's family.

Parker looks over at me. "Are you sure you don't want to pay your respects?" he asks, quietly.

"Not now." I will, but I'm not ready to say goodbye in front of all these strangers.

The organ begins, sending chills down my spine. I know some people find it beautiful, but something about the haunting music makes me uneasy.

When it's time for the eulogy, I'm surprised to see Brandon stand. "Good morning. Thank you all for being here today and helping Ethan and me celebrate Amy's life. Amy and I met in college. Some would call it love at first sight, and others would call it a game of cat and mouse. I was the cat."

A few people laugh quietly. "Amy saw nothing but good in the world and in those around her. She was always happy and proud of the life she lived, the woman she had become, and the family she created. Everything she did was for Ethan and me. There was no decision she made lightly, and she always made the time for what mattered most to her. The world is missing a great woman, but today isn't about her loss, or saying goodbye. Amy didn't want that. Today is about celebrating her life. She'll be missed by her family and friends, and most of all by our amazing son."

He pauses, looking over at the casket. "Amy, baby, I promise to watch over him, guide him into to a fine young man, and stand by his side proudly. I'll support him, love him, and tell him every single day how much his mommy loved him. There won't be a day that you won't be thought of. I love you."

He steps down and wipes away his tears. His speech was sweet and simple, but it was spot on.

Parker takes my hand. There are tears in his eyes, and I gently wipe them away.

The rest of the funeral is nice—well, as nice as a funeral can be. Even though I only knew Amy for a short time, it feels like she's always been a part of my life.

I watch cars driving away from the cemetery as I sit in the cool dirt. Parker stepped away, giving me space to say goodbye.

I run my hands through the dirt, trying to find a coherent thought. "I'm not sure what I'll do without you. I feel as if I've lost a part of myself. Every time I saw you, you were stronger than the time before and that was such an inspiration to me. You had this aura around you. This amazing ability to see the good in everything, no matter the hurt or pain. You always saw the beauty. I don't think I can bring myself to say goodbye because, when it comes to our friendship, I don't think goodbye is for us."

"Aundrea?"

Startled, I turn to see Brandon blocking the sunlight.

"Brandon."

"Thank you for coming today."

I look down at my empty hands. "Of course."

He holds out an envelope. "Amy wrote this for you and asked that I give it to you when she passed."

"Thank you," I choke, taking the paper from him.

He turns away from me and I call after him. "Brandon?"

"Yeah?"

"I'm sorry."

"Thank you." He gives me a smile. It's small, but it's there. "It's okay. I'll be okay. I grieved in March when we realized there was nothing more we could do. I've had the last few months to come to terms with the pain and enjoy the time with my wife. I got to grieve with her, which helped. So … Aundrea? I'm sorry for *your* loss. I'm sorry she didn't tell you and you didn't get to grieve with her. To celebrate her life with her."

My eyes flutter closed and fresh tears streak my face. When I'm left alone I open the letter with trembling hands.

Aundrea,

If you're reading this, you know, and I wish I could have told you. Please believe me when I tell you I tried many times, but telling you wouldn't have made any of this easier.

I never told you about stopping treatment because I didn't want to feed your fear. I didn't want you to see my life in a negative way because it's been nothing but beautiful to me. I got something most people don't get when they're faced with death. I got time. I was able to plan and spend time with my loved ones. We were able to prepare and I'll be forever thankful for the time I got with them.

People take life for granted. They don't stop to smell

the flowers for no reason, or dance around in the rain because they're happy. Being alive is a lot more than breathing every day. It's savoring every moment. It's getting in as many experiences as you can in the time you have. You don't know what you have, or what's missing, until it's gone. Life is too short. Too short to think about everything that scares you. Too short to wonder what you could be doing, rather than doing it. Too short for regrets.

I don't believe in chance encounters. I believe people come into our life for a specific reason and that we met so that we could help one another. Learn from each other. I needed you just as much as you needed me, and no words will ever be able to describe how thankful I am for your friendship. I don't regret one second with you, Aundrea. My life is far from over. It's just beginning, as is yours. Don't let go of your dreams. Go after them and have hope. You're going to get through this and go on to live a long, healthy life with your beautiful family. With your child.

Never be afraid, Aundrea. Life is never guaranteed and you need to enjoy what you have no matter what. I'll always be with you. Please don't doubt yourself. You're so strong, Aundrea. Remember that.

Yours forever,
Amy

Unable to move, I sit there, clutching the letter. I feel so weak. Amy once called me her angel, but really she's been mine. And I'll continue to think of her as my guardian angel.

Parker's hand lightly brushes my shoulder. "Are you ready?"

I glance down at the letter. Life is so unpredictable. It will always be difficult, given my history. Fear will sometimes creep in; get me down. But unless I get back up, I'll never know if I can defeat it. Amy is right. Living a life not ruled by fear is difficult, but I have Parker standing by my side, helping me. And that makes it so much easier.

It's time I break down the walls I've built. Cancer will always be a part of who I am, no matter how much it sucks or hurts. There's no way around it, nor is there any point in running from it, but it doesn't define who I am as a person.

Pain is what keeps my heart alive.

Pain is a reminder of the life I have to be thankful for.

Aundrea

efore I know it, we're in the heart of the July heat. I
haven't gone back to volunteering at Mayo yet. I know
Amy would want me to, but I'm not quite ready.

Parker's birthday is the last weekend in July and I decided
to surprise him with a weekend up north in Brainerd at a
small resort on the lake. I thought we could use the time
away.

The morning of our first full day here, and Parker's
birthday, the warm morning sun shines through our room,
illuminating everything in sight. It's peaceful being here.
Every worry feels a million miles away. It's just the two of
us—no social media, work, family, or problems to get in the
way.

I finish my make-up and slip into a colorful sundress, the
cotton soft against my skin.

Parker has on plaid blue and white swim shorts and
white T-shirt with a surfer standing next to a blue surfboard,
which reads, "SAVE A WAVE, RIDE A SURFER."

"I hope that shirt is intended for me?" I smirk.

"Of, course. Just a friendly reminder that I'm available all
day and night if you need a good ride."

"If?"

"When, *when* you need a good ride."

I give him one of his own winks and blow him a kiss. I tie my hair back in a low bun, slip on my sunglasses, and nod to Parker that I'm ready.

As we eat breakfast I notice that Parker is watching me with interest.

"What?" I ask.

"I was just watching you. And thinking that if we have a boy, I hope he's into cars like his dad."

I laugh. "And if we have a girl?"

"I hope she's as beautiful as her mother."

"I just care that he or she is healthy."

Parker looks at me strangely.

"I used to laugh when expectant parents said that. I mean, what parent wouldn't hope for that? Everyone says it, but now … it has so much more meaning to me."

"I want that too, babe."

Suddenly, everything my parents and Genna ever did for me growing up and going through treatment makes complete sense, including my mom's constant worry and Genna's hovering when I lived with her briefly. I get it. It never ends.

"I'll do everything I can to protect our child, Parker. To take all their pain away. I promise."

"I believe you."

I lean over the table and cup his face lightly in my hands. "I love you."

⸉ ⌒ ⌒ ⸊

When the time comes for our first OB appointment, I drive so Parker can have a couple of hours to relax. He's been working extra hard at the clinic, taking on more hours. We're trying hard to avoid taking out a loan.

I don't think I allowed him much relaxation, though, with the radio blaring and my off key singing to every pop song that plays. My parents didn't bless me with a great singing voice, even though I like to pretend it's out of this world.

When Parker looks out of the corner of his eye at me, I pick up the car charger cord and bring it to my lips. When I begin to sing into it as if it's a microphone, he breaks into a laughing fit. It isn't before long I'm joining his laughter.

I start to wish I hadn't driven as we enter downtown Minneapolis. There are way too many one-ways making it extremely confusing to navigate.

My stress turns into excitement when we pull into the parking lot and Parker stretches his legs, grinning at me from behind his Ray Bans. I'm so excited for this appointment.

My yellow sundress blows in the wind as we walk side by side, our fingers locked together. We don't say a word as we enter the building.

Wendy's already in the lobby and she stands when she sees us. She's wearing a tight tank top and, to the average person, she wouldn't look like she's pregnant, but to me, it's clear as day. Her once-flat stomach has a little more shape to it, and it's an amazing feeling to know it's our baby inside of her. Up until now, it hasn't seemed real. It's easy to forget that we're expecting a child when we have nothing to see each day.

"Hey, you two!" Wendy beams. She's glowing. Her smile is bright and stunning.

"Hi." I have an urge to reach out and touch her stomach, but don't want to seem creepy.

"Hey, how are you feeling?" Parker asks. I can tell by the way he clutches his fingers that he has the same urge as me.

"Great! It's crazy because I haven't had any morning sickness with this pregnancy. If it weren't for starting to show, I wouldn't even know I was pregnant!"

"You look fantastic, Wendy," I say.

Wendy hugs Parker and me. Before we even sit down, her name is called.

"Wendy Henderson?"

The nurse looks momentarily surprised that there are

three of us, but I'm sure she's dealt with surrogates before.

In the exam room, the nurse takes Wendy's vitals, then leaves us alone.

Wendy's sitting on the exam table with her ankles crossed when Parker asks, "Are you sure it's okay I'm here?" I can tell he's nervous because he's running a hand through his hair, and I giggle. Parker's not easily bashful, but apparently all it takes is taking another woman to a doctor's appointment. I find this shy side of him sexy.

Wendy grins. "Of course, Parker. Don't be silly. I want the two of you to be very much involved in this entire process. Trust me."

We're soon interrupted by a light knock on the door.

"Well, good afternoon!" The doctor says. I glance at my watch. This has to be the shortest time I've ever waited to see a doctor. Like, *Guinness Book of World Records* book short.

Parker and I both sit up straight and I shake the doctor's hand.

Dr. Martin is older, maybe in his early fifties, and tall. He seems nice and the way he jokes around puts me at ease. He was the doctor who did the implantation and all three of us agreed to continue seeing him. He makes us all feel comfortable.

"All right, we're at ten weeks," Dr. Martin says. Since learning of her pregnancy every day has flown by. It's hard to believe it's already August.

"Let's find a heartbeat, shall we?"

As Wendy lies back, Parker wraps his arm around my waist, pulling me closer.

"You can hear it this early?" I ask, amazed. I'd looked online and ten weeks is about the size of kumquat. *Tiny.*

"Ten weeks is the earliest you can. Now, the fetus is pretty low at this stage, so I'll need you to lower your pants a little more for me."

Parker looks away at first, but the second the loud, racing thumps from the fetal Doppler begin, he looks back. His hold on me tightens. We're both staring at Wendy's stomach in awe.

"Is that really …" I know it is, but hearing it still shocks me. I think my own heart just burst.

"Sure is. Strong, too," Dr. Martin says.

"That's amazing," Parker stammers.

"Is it supposed to be that fast?" I ask, looking at the doctor. I have no idea what's normal, but the Doppler is showing well over 160 beats per minute, and I know an adult heart can't function at that speed.

"Yes, babe. It's perfect," Parker answers, taking my hand and giving my palm a lingering kiss.

It's magical that something so tiny can produce such a strong sound. Tears of happiness sting my eyes. This is probably the best sound I've ever heard. That little heart is beating because of us. The thumps grow stronger and I swallow the lump in my throat.

Parker and I look at Wendy and then each other. No words are needed. We can see it on our faces. This bond will connect us forever.

Our baby.

chapter

EIGHTEEN

Parker

"Hey, Parker?" Jason says, pushing open my office door. "You ready?"

"Yeah, I'll meet you there." We agreed to have a men's taco poker night. It's been a while since the guys have gotten together to drink beer, eat tacos, and play cards. Since the girls are having dinner and going to the movies, it seemed like the perfect opportunity.

I arrive at Jason's just before six to find Kevin and Jason at the kitchen table with two men I've never met and Hannah in her bouncy chair, playing quietly. Sometimes I wonder if people even know Jason and Genna have a baby, because she's always so content, happy, and quiet.

"Hey, Parker! Grab a beer and pull up a seat. This is Rob and Tony. They live a few houses down from me," Kevin slurs. Clearly, he didn't work today and got a head start on the beers.

"Hey guys. Nice to meet you." I take a Bud Light out of the fridge and sit down.

"You too," they say. They're about my age: early thirties.

"And, you know Brandon," Jason says, taking his seat.

I give Brandon a handshake. "How are you?"

"Doing well, man. Thanks."

"Okay, ladies. You going to sit and talk or play some poker?" Kevin grumbles playfully. "You're going to need to bring your game if we want to force Jackson to trade in that fancy car of his for a minivan."

"Let me be clear right now," I say. "I will *not* be driving a minivan. Not now or in the future. Never. The FRS is capable of holding a car seat just fine. Besides, Aundrea has her Outlander for the family vehicle."

Jason starts laughing.

"What?" I ask, glaring at him.

"I said the same thing. But little did I know that Genna had other plans and traded her G6 in for a damn van. I swore I'd never be caught driving one of those."

"Trust me when I tell you, I won't be driving a van. Besides, you're whipped," I taunt.

"Whipped?" Jason looks shocked.

"Yeah, pussy whipped!" Kevin agrees, laughing.

Tony and Rob start laughing, too, but then Tony says that he and his fiancée have a van for their two kids and they actually love it. He goes on and on about the room it has and how smoothly it drives.

This does nothing to convince me.

"As much as I love talking about cars, I hate talking about minivans. Let's get back to playing some poker," I say. I'm ready to take these guys to the cleaners.

Sometime in the middle of our game, after Rob, Brandon and Kevin are out, Jason puts Hannah to bed. I check my phone to see if I have a text from Aundrea and, since I don't, I decide to send her one.

Me: *How's ladies night going?*

The Wife: *Hey, you. It's going good! The movie just let out. We're thinking of going to get some drinks. There's a bar here doing happy hour until 11.*

Me: *Sounds fun. May I suggest getting really drunk so I can take advantage of you later?*

The Wife: *No need to take advantage, handsome. I'm more than willing.*

Me: *In that case, get ready.*

The Wife: *Will do. How's poker?*

Me: *Good. Down to Jason, the new guy, and myself. I'm about to take them for everything they've got.*

The Wife: *Good, Momma needs a new pair of shoes!!*

I chuckle at her comment. She's not a shoe girl. Sending her one last text, I put my phone away.

"What? We're talking to our women now on guy's night?" Kevin teases.

"Just wait until Jean moves in. If you don't check in with her, she'll be all over your ass."

"Nah. Jean's not like that. That's why I love her. She doesn't care what I do."

"Dude, that's because you don't live together. It's not affecting her at all," Jason insists.

"Shit," Kevin mumbles.

I laugh, but immediately cringe when my eyes meet Brandon's. He's smiling faintly, but his eyes are hard. I wasn't thinking how difficult it could be for him to hear us joking around like this, fronting like our lovers are a hardship instead of a blessing.

"What is going on with the moving in together situation, anyway?" Tony asks.

"Nothing. She vetoed that. She likes how things are." Kevin runs his hand along his jaw. "I hate to admit this … and don't any of you fuckers laugh." He downs his beer. "I feel like I'm the damn woman in this relationship! I practically begged her to move in with me and she turned me down. I even said I love you first."

"And you said *I'm* pussy whipped? Man, you're so much more than I am!" Jason shouts, laughing.

Even Brandon smiles at that.

I kind of feel bad for the Kevin. I can tell how much he loves Jean and wants to be with her. I can even see that Jean cares for Kevin, but I know from Aundrea that Jean isn't a woman to change her life for a man.

"All in due time. She's young; remember that," I say. I think he forgets sometimes that he's thirty-two and she's only twenty-four.

"Aundrea's young and look at you two; married and shit, with a baby on the way."

"Like you said, Jean's different."

We finish the game. I don't win, but I come in second, which is still a chunk of change.

"All right, guys. It's been fun, but I'm out of here."

"Me too," Brandon adds, standing up.

"You going to go poke Aundrea's taco? Get it? Taco poker night? Poke her taco?" Kevin laughs at his own joke and I can only manage to shake my head and shrug apologetically at Brandon, who waves it off, laughing.

Jason smacks the back of Kevin's head, and Rob and Tony laugh with him.

Brandon and I don't wait to say goodbye. We walk out to our cars together, in silence.

I'm not sure what to say. We haven't spoken since the funeral. Aundrea called him a couple times, inviting him and Ethan over but he's yet to come by.

"It's been fun," Brandon says.

"Yeah, it was. Listen, if you're free and want to come by again, we'd like that."

"I would too. I don't get out much, lately."

"How are you doing?"

Leaning against his car, he scrubs his hands over his face.

"It's been hard."

"You and Ethan are welcome over any time."

"I know that, thanks. We're just trying to figure things out … the two of us. Ethan's taken it a lot harder than I thought he would. I guess I really didn't know how he would take it. He cries every night for her." His words sound strangled. "I can get through my pain, but I didn't think how difficult it would be to take away his."

I don't know what to say to that. How do you take away the pain of a child who lost their mother? Will time make it better?

"I gave him a picture of her. He said it's not the same. I know where he's coming from, but I can only hope it helps."

"It does. Even if he doesn't say it, it does."

He nods.

"How are *you* doing?" He hasn't really mentioned if he's okay. He looks it, but I want to make sure he is.

"Each day gets better. They say time heals all wounds. I believe that. I miss her smell the most. I didn't think about how much I would miss that until she was gone." He sighs heavily, looking over my shoulder. "I better get going."

He closes his eyes, not looking at my nod of understanding. "See you."

He gets into his car and says through the window, "Talk to you soon, Parker."

I drive home at the slowest speed I have ever driven.

Aundrea's already asleep, her hair slightly damp from a shower.

I crawl into the warm sheets and pull her against me, taking in her scent. I hope to never forget this smell. Pears and honey. My favorite smell in the entire world.

Breathing her in, I drift off to sleep.

"Breathe!" I scream, looking down at her face. She jerks with each movement.

19, 20, 21, 22, 23, 24, 25, 26

Come on, Aundrea! Breathe!"

I jolt awake. I'm covered in cold sweat and tears are streaming down my face, but when I roll over Aundrea is still sleeping peacefully.

I rub my hand over my face, as if I could scrub the visions away. I need them to be gone. I can't stand the thought of Aundrea's lifeless body. My hands tremble as the memories wash over me again.

I grunt in annoyance and frustration as I focus on the woman sleeping before me. I listen to her breathe and pull her back against my chest, so I can feel her warmth against me. I need her warmth.

Fuck, why are they starting again? It's been a while since I've had that dream. They started when I learned of Aundrea's heart condition, but stopped after a few months.

Nothing comes into mind except …

Fuck.

My conversation with Brandon.

This damned dream has brought out the one thing I try to keep hidden. It's the only thing in my life I'm not proud of. Even though Aundrea's cancer free, it terrifies me that her cardiomyopathy could take her at any moment. No matter how many appointments I go to, test results I see, or pills I watch her take every morning, it's a thought I just can't shake. I'd do anything for this woman. Anything. But there's nothing I can do about her condition.

I close my eyes, trying my best to leave the nightmare behind. But it's difficult to leave something so haunting … so terrifying, behind you.

I hate that in the dream I can't protect her. I can't save her.

Even though I vowed that I would.

I hate that dream.

"Parker?" Aundrea's voice is like sunshine breaking through the dark cloud of thoughts.

"I'm okay."

"No, you're not. You're soaking wet. Come here. You're okay, shh," she whispers, running her fingers through my hair. I like when she comforts me; I just hate that I need it.

Throwing the drenched sheets off me, I pull Aundrea onto my chest, so she's lying flat against me. I can't get her close enough.

"Stop," she whispers in my ear.

I take in the alluring scent of fresh shampoo from our shower last night mixed with a hint of coconut from her lotion.

"Stop what?" I ask, drawing circles on her smooth bare back.

"Thinking about it."

I close my eyes tightly, forcing myself to stay here, in this moment.

She lays her head on my shoulder and wraps her arms around my waist, hugging me. Softly, she says, "What do I need to do, or say, to make you understand that I'm not going to leave you?"

I take a deep breath and let it out slowly. "I don't know, Aundrea. I believe you, but I can't seem to shake the feeling that one day I'm going to wake up, and you won't be here. That I'll be forced to face the world without you, and I can't do that. I've never been more afraid of anything in my life."

I think of Brandon. How he looked. The pain in his eyes when he spoke of Ethan. It breaks me.

She looks down at me. Tips of her blonde hair brush my face and I shiver. "Remember when you told me you saw my future?"

I nod.

"Well, I see it too. I am your future Parker. This" — she gestures between us — "is real. We're real. Not that dream. I took a vow, 'From here through eternity, for death will not separate us.' Death will *not* take me away from you, Parker. I won't let it."

Swallowing hard, I take her face between my hands, pulling her toward me until our lips almost touch.

"There is no life if it's not a life with you," I whisper against her mouth before giving her the lightest of kisses.

I tug her hair gently as I deepen the kiss. I need to feel her touch.

Her existence.

Her love.

I wrap her in my arms and roll her beneath me. I run my hands up and down her arms until I feel her goosebumps. She watches me intently as I reach for the bottom of her shirt and lift it up over her head.

Our mouths join almost immediately, slow and sensual, as our hands roam. We undress one another, never breaking apart. We take our time, enjoying every moment.

When I enter her, her hands find mine and we lock eyes.

"I love you so much, Aundrea."

"Ditto."

Slowly we begin to move in an effortless dance.

I make love to my wife, showing her just how much I need her.

⁓ C ℭ ⁓

Aundrea's not back when I get home just after seven the following evening. I had an emergency walk-in, so I let her know I'd be late. She texted me back immediately saying she was going out with Shannon and would see me when she got back.

When eight o'clock hits I lie down on the couch to catch up on some TV, but instead drift off to sleep.

"Come on, Aundrea! Breathe!"
27, 28, 29, 30
Breathe.
Breathe.

"Come on, baby. Come on!" I scream so loud that I jolt myself awake.

What the fuck is happening?

I look around our empty living room, the TV screen black.

I fell asleep. The clock reads 9:03pm.

The temperature has dropped, and I'm shivering. The room feels empty without Aundrea here, as if her absence has sucked away all the life. I know this feeling.

And I hate it.

Hesitating, I sit up. I know I don't want to go back to sleep. There's no point in trying. Not right now.

Not without her here. I know what will happen the second I drift off. My head begins to feel heavy and my throat feels tight at the thought of that dream.

I look at my phone. One missed call and one text from Aundrea from about twenty minutes ago.

> The Wife: *We ended up running into a friend of Shannon's and decided to stay for dinner. Sorry! I'm leaving now. See you soon.*

I take a couple of deep breaths, but it almost feels like I'm under water and can't come up for air.

Death.

It's haunting me.

Toying with my emotions.

Slumping to the floor, I rest my back against our white couch. I'm too hot, now, and I'm sweating, drenching my black collared shirt. I'm sticking to the couch, but I don't bother peeling myself off. I'm not giving in tonight. I won't let the helplessness take over. I refuse to give into that fog.

Time slowly passes by. I can't say for certain how long I've been sitting here with nothing but the ticking of each passing second and the flashing low battery signal on my cell. My eyes feel heavy, but I refuse to let them close.

"Parker?" *Aundrea.* Her voice is faint, concerned even. "Are you okay?"

There's a small break in her voice when she says "okay," which is when I look up to see her standing before me in jeans and a plain white shirt. She took her hair out of the ponytail she was wearing this morning.

"You're home." I'm relieved enough to finally allow my eyes to close briefly.

"What's the matter?" She crouches down to look into my eyes.

I sigh.

Her head drops slightly, her eyes close, and her mouth settles into a straight line.

I'm panting now. My heart is beating a mile a minute, pounding louder as I concentrate on my surroundings.

"Parker." She steps around me to sit on the couch, pulling me back to rest between her legs.

Her right hand rests on my head and her left curls around my shoulder, embracing me. She doesn't pay any attention to my soaked clothes. Before I can say anything, she presses her cheek against my hair. Then her lips come down, brushing against my scalp in a tender kiss.

I close my eyes at her touch, and lean back. "You are my end, Aundrea." I'm trembling. "I can't … I—I … you." I pause, licking my lips. "I can't watch you die anymore. I can't …" I trail off, my voice barely there.

I wrap my right arm around her knee, holding her in place. I don't want her to move. I need the closeness.

"I know, shh. I'm right here." She squeezes me gently.

I feel her slump heavily against me.

"Babe?" My voice cracks. "Help me. Please save me from drowning."

She squeezes her arms around me. We're both shaking.

"There isn't anything I wouldn't do for you, Parker."

"I never want to leave your side. Not in life, not after, not even in my dreams. I want you next to me. How do I let that go?"

Aundrea loosens her grip and comes to face me, dropping to her knees.

"Parker, I can't change the past and I can't control the future. I can control the present, but I can't do it without you. I may be your end, but you are my beginning. Every part of you *and* our child. I'll do whatever it takes to show you that our life is far from over. We're just getting started, you me—and, soon, our baby. We're far from being done. I'm far from gone."

I take her hand and gently tug her closer. I can see her confidence—that she truly believes her words—and it makes it easier to be comforted. My head is spinning like a carnival ride I can't get off.

Aundrea takes a deep breath and I prepare myself for her next words. "I'm going to die, Parker. We're all going to. I am going to leave my loved ones behind, as will you some day. It may not be cancer or my heart, but something *will* take me away from you one day. The sooner you accept that, the sooner you can move forward. I've recently had to accept this myself. Amy told me that getting over a fear doesn't happen overnight, but accepting that fear will let you begin to overcome it."

"Have you gotten over yours?"

"I'm trying, Parker. Lord knows I'm trying. As much as leaving you or our child behind scares me, I'm doing my best to face it. I'm not sure the fear will ever go away completely. But let me try to help you. Like you said, we're in it together. This is no different. We'll confront our fears together."

I cup her face, brushing her hair behind her ear. "I love the sound of your voice." My lips meet hers. "Your curves." I squeeze her hips, pulling her onto my lap. "The freckles on your nose." I graze her cheek. "And the scars on your innocent skin." I leave a trail of kisses down her neck. "God, and your smell." I sigh into the crook of her neck.

"Remember when you told me that we can take on the world together?"

"Yes," I choke out.

"Well, I believe you. I need you to believe it too. I need you to open your eyes and see what's in front of you." She leans back, holding my gaze. "Amy told me once that we need to stay strong. We need to look forward, no matter what, not back. Look forward with me."

"I'm looking." I keep looking into her big hazel eyes that

are pleading with me.

"I'm here, by your side, and I'm not going anywhere. This is reality, Parker. Not your nightmare. It's you, me and our baby. I need you to let it go. Let it go and see the light that's here."

I don't cry often. I tend to bottle up my emotions, tuck them away where they never see daylight. But Aundrea's brought out a side of me I never knew existed. She's made me a better man—a man capable of conquering any obstacle. I've never loved like this. She and I … we were made to love one another.

"You were sent for me. With everything I am, I know there is no love stronger than ours. You need to let go. Let go and fight for us," she whispers, bringing her lips against mine.

"I am!" I practically yell. I immediately lower my voice, pleading for her to understand. "Aundrea, I fight for you every day. And in that dream … I fight for that one breath of air. One damn breath. If I could only reach you in time to give it to you." I stop. I can't finish. All I can see is her cold hand in mine, and all I can hear is the cracking of her ribs as I crush the chest of the woman I love giving her CPR.

My heart pounds. I close my eyes and swallow. Try to force myself not to cry, but my eyes start to burn anyway. Not able to fight it any longer, tears begin to fall and Aundrea wipes them away. "Aundrea, I fight for you every day. To have a life with you. A future. I want to give you everything I can."

I'm terrified.

Terrified I can't make all her dreams come true.

Terrified I'll let her down.

Terrified I'll lose her.

"And you are. Now I need you to fight that fear. Face it. With me."

"Is that what you did?"

"What do you mean?"

"By marrying me? By deciding to have a baby?"

She shakes her head. "No, I should have never said those awful things to you at the hospital. Marrying you and having a baby isn't what scares me. It's the possibility that the cancer will come back, or my heart will stop. I feel every blood draw I give or body scan I do is a constant reminder of what could be lost. That one day I could be taken away from you or our child, forcing you two to go on without me. That I won't get to see our little one grow up, or that I won't get to grow old with you. That's my fear. But I'm learning to face it. I needed to explore it and accept it because if I didn't it would control my life. I'm done with outside forces controlling my life, so I'm facing it. I'm looking my fear in the eye. Together, we'll conquer it all. You've never talked me into doing anything. Everything I do is because I want it. I want to be your wife and grow old with you. I want to have a lot of babies with you, Parker Cade Jackson."

"And how do you propose I face my fear?"

"Accept it. Fear will always be around us, Parker. It's what we do with that fear that matters. You need to stop running. Show it that it can no longer control you. Once it's confronted, it will lose its hold on you."

"Just like that?"

She gives me a sad smile. "I can't control that I was sick. I can't control my current state of health, but together we can control the path our life takes. Living a life based on fear isn't living at all. Those words are sticking to me like glue. If we accept that someday I'm going to pass on, that *you're* going to pass on, then we can move on and continue to live our life together, as a family."

I pull her to my chest, clutching her tightly. "I'm scared, Aundrea. Scared of living without you. Scared of that nightmare becoming reality. I don't want to end up like Brandon. I'm terrified of finding you one day ... God, I can't watch it again."

"Me too." She sighs into my chest. "Me too." Her soft fingers rub soothing circles on my back.

She places my right hand on her chest, and my left

on my own and covers my hands with hers. I can feel the strong, steady beating of her heart, as if it's speaking its own language. "Do you feel this?" I nod. I feel it loud and clear. "My heart beats as long as yours does. We're one, Parker. I'm not going anywhere without you. We're unbreakable."

I believe her. With all of me, I believe everything that comes out of her mouth. I'm just not convinced she believes what she's saying. Not convinced that her fear will dissipate in the face of her words.

"I don't want to be without you," I whisper.

"You never will be."

I run my finger along her cheekbone and across her chin. Her eyes close at my touch. I kiss each closed lid. "You have such a beautiful heart."

The love I have for her is something I know she'll never fully understand. The love *we* have is something most people only wish to experience. She is my present, my future, and my eternity. I won't let fear wreck what we have.

It's time I face it.

It's time I give her that breath.

chapter

NINETEEN

Aundrea

"I'm home!" I yell excitedly when I get home.

I set my purse down and walk into the empty living room. "Parker?"

I flip on the light in the kitchen. No sign of life.

I didn't work at the clinic today because, for some reason I have yet to figure out, Genna managed to talk me into helping her pick out and test new recipes today.

Parker said the guys had meetings all day so their schedules were pretty light and it'd be okay to take the day off.

I glance at the clock. Just after four. Parker said he'd be home early, so I can only assume he's running behind. I don't have any texts or missed calls.

My feet are cramped from being on them all day. I pull off my shoes and socks and eagerly swap them for my fluffy pink slippers, relaxing the moment my feet sink into softness. I go upstairs to take a quick shower. My shoulders are tense and I'm more than eager to wash away the long day.

Taped on the mirror is a handwritten note from Parker:

Aundrea,

If I've planned this correctly, you should

have approximately thirty minutes to change and get yourself outside. There will be a limo waiting for you out front that will take you to meet me. I can't wait to see you.

I love you.
Parker

I stop reading. *What is this man up to now?* I'm completely confused. I think about what day it is, but can't come up with any important event we'd be celebrating tonight.

I rip the letter off the mirror, taking it with me, and run over to our closet, all thoughts of relaxing gone. I stare blankly at my closet. How is it I have so many clothes but nothing to wear? I don't think I have anything in my closet fancy enough for wherever I'd be going in a limo.

Looking back at the letter, I finish reading.

P.S. Don't stress. You'll look great in whatever you choose.
P.P.S. If I did not plan this correctly, then you would have seen the limo in our driveway and must be very confused. In that case, hurry your sweet ass up and get back downstairs, as that limo is waiting for you.
wink

I drop the note. Genna's manipulations make sense now. Of *course* she'd be in on this.

At lightning speed, I shuffle through hangers, deciding on a short, layered, strapless black dress. Feeling the ultra-soft fabric, I smile and slip it on.

I give myself a once over in the mirror. The dress clings to me perfectly and flows over my hips, the bottom layer ending mid-thigh while the sheer top layer hangs just past my knees.

Quickly touching up my make-up and fixing my hair, I spray on perfume so I won't smell like I've been cooking all day.

The ache in my feet disappears as I slip on a pair of black lace flats with square jewels on the toes. I grab my purse, lock the door behind me, and practically skip down the driveway.

True to Parker's word, there is a black limo waiting at the curb. I carefully walk to a chauffeur who's dressed in all black, with a fancy hat on his hairless head.

"Good evening, Mrs. Jackson. I'm Craig. I'll be your driver this evening."

"Hello." I give him a shy smile.

Craig opens the door for me and I climb into the back.

"You'll find a bottle of wine in the chiller and a remote for the radio. Feel free to listen to anything you like. It won't be a long ride."

"Are we picking up Parker?"

"No, ma'am. Mr. Jackson will be meeting you at our final destination." *Final destination?*

With those words, he rolls up the glass partition.

I pour myself a glass of wine and lean back against the leather cushion. I can't seem to stop smiling as I text Parker.

Me: *What are you up to?*

He responds immediately.

Mr. Handsome: *Wait until you see.*

I shake my head. Parker loves surprises and he enjoys giving them to me any chance he can get.

It's not long before the limo comes to a stop at . . . Max's Bar?

"What the?" I mumble.

Craig opens my door and holds out his hand to help me out.

"What are we doing here?"

There's a small crowd outside smoking and, from the wide eyes and confused looks I'm getting, I assume my entrance is a little extravagant for what's going on inside.

"Mr. Jackson has asked that I escort you inside."

Confused, I follow Craig into the bar. The place is pretty packed for an early weekday evening, and music is already blaring.

The hostess greets me.

I start to speak, but Craig says, "This is Mrs. Jackson."

"Oh, Aundrea!" she says excitedly, bouncing on her heels as if she's been expecting me all night.

"That's me," I reply, nonplussed. I glance around at the crowd, looking for Parker.

"Here, I'm supposed to give this to you." She hands me a single long-stemmed yellow rose and a folded piece of paper.

I take them from her with a shaky hand. I'm not sure why, but this entire situation has me on edge.

Opening the note, I read:

> Aundrea,
>
> My life changed here. It was the night I met the love of my life. You. I don't think I'll ever be able to fully describe what you have done to me, but always know the beginning of us started here.
>
> Parker

I look up to see the hostess smiling widely.

"Is he here?" I ask, scanning the crowd over her shoulder.

She shakes her head. "No, I'm sorry."

"Mrs. Jackson, if you'll come with me," Craig says from behind me.

I follow him back out to the limo. I read the note over and over again as we drive. Soon we come to another stop, the door opens, and Craig holds his hand out for me again.

The building before us is all too familiar. I don't wait for Craig to open the door; I just jog up the steps of our old apartment building. The night security guard, Neil, is standing there with a huge, happy grin.

"Evening, Mrs. Jackson."

"Hi Neil."

He hands me a single yellow rose and a note.

Aundrea,

When you walked out of my life, I was certain I'd never see you again. I can't explain it, but you exerted this gravitational pull on me (and still do). I craved your attention, needed your touch, and wanted nothing more than to hear your voice again. There was something special about you that ignited a yearning within me. My prayers were answered that night at Jason's house when we were brought face to face again.
Even though this building is part of our past, it will always be the start our future.

Parker

The butterflies in my stomach are fluttering so strongly I'm almost convinced they're real.

"Are we going to see him soon?" I ask Craig.

"Soon. One more stop." He closes the limo door behind me, leaving me to ponder.

After what feels like an eternity, we pull up to Graham Arena—the ice arena where we once went on a date. I don't wait for Craig to open the door. I jump out of the limo and walk into the building, memories of us ice-skating coming back to me. I'm not sure where I'm going, but I check with the counter first.

"Hello, my name is Aundrea." I pause, looking for Parker. "I'm looking—"

"For this?" The young man pulls out a note and another yellow rose.

"That." I nod and take it from him.

> Aundrea,
>
> This is where I fell in love with you. I couldn't take my eyes off you as you skated around the arena, laughing and smiling. I didn't just see a woman on the ice, I saw the woman I was going to marry. I admire you, Aundrea. Each and every day, I admire the strength you have and your willingness to keep moving forward.
>
> Parker

I'm sobbing before I even finish the note. I never knew the exact moment Parker fell in love with me. They say that when you know, you just know. It turns out Parker knew from the very beginning that we were meant to be together.

I have no idea what is going on. I don't know why Parker felt the sudden need for these notes, or what he is up to, but I do know I have never felt so much emotion run through me as a result of so few words. I'm blown away by the affection, love, and admiration he feels for me.

Tears stream down my face and I clutch the note to my chest. I walk eagerly back to the limo, needing more than anything to see Parker.

The ride to our final destination is short. I don't recognize anything as we pass buildings, landscapes, and houses. When we turn down a dark, secluded road, I go rigid.

Where in the world are we going?

Soon, twinkle lights come into view and, as we draw nearer, I see Parker standing alone in front of a gazebo. We're in the middle of nowhere, surrounded by nothing but green grass.

Seeing him standing there, I almost feel like I'm on an episode of *The Bachelor*, with the limo pulling up and the gorgeous man waiting for each woman to step out.

Craig helps me out and I practically run to Parker, smiling wider all the way.

"Hi," I whisper, reaching him. My eyes are already misty and he hasn't even spoken yet. Just looking at him sends my emotions all over the place. He's wearing nice dress pants and a red button-down.

"Hi back." He gives me the charming smile I love so much and leans in, giving me a lingering kiss on the lips.

"What's going on?"

Behind us, in the lighted gazebo, a table is set for two. In the grass, a blanket is laid out with a telescope.

I hear the crunching of tires at the limo pulls away.

"Aundrea, recently you've reminded me that it doesn't matter what happens in life, as long as we live it together. It's not about fear, doubt, or failure. It's about being together and embracing what's important. These last few months have been crazy and tonight I wanted to give you—or, rather, *us*—a night where nothing else in the world matters."

"Parker."

"You've yet to teach me about astronomy so I thought, what better time than now? So, I've gotten us a high tech telescope that I can't figure out how to use and dinner for two." He holds his hands out in a proud gesture, and I laugh.

"Well then, handsome, let's get to it."

I show him how to set up the Celestron telescope, even though I know he'll never remember how to align it again.

We nibble on pizza as I locate different planets and stars, giving Parker a short history of each.

Later, we end up lying on the blanket, just staring at the sky. It's dark and clear. There's no sound around us, just the two of us enjoying the warm, quiet evening.

It's impossible to count all the stars, of course, but as I lie here, snuggled against Parker, I try.

"Why do they twinkle?" Parker asks. He takes the hand I'm pointing as I try to count.

"I love when they twinkle." I stop counting and look at my Mr. Handsome. How far we've come to feel so complete. He looks young as he waits for my reply.

"There's turbulence in the atmosphere that causes a star's light to refract in different directions, which makes it look dimmer and then brighter. So it looks like it twinkles."

Parker turns onto his side, brushing the hair off my face, and kisses my forehead.

"I love the stars," I say. "The universe is such a beautiful thing to study. It's like trying to piece together a story. Putting chapters of its life together, just like ours. You never know what you're going to learn or encounter. Like life, there is still so much to know."

"Like us."

"Like us." I confirm. "You know, they say true love exists in the stars."

"They do?" Parker raises an eyebrow, smirking.

"Of course. I mean, if you believe in astrology."

Parker grins. "Continue."

"Us, for example. I'm a Pisces, a water sign, and you're a Leo, a fire sign. You put the two together and you have nothing but steam."

"One would think water and fire wouldn't mix well?" he counters.

"Well, Leos like being center stage. They can help a shy Piscean overcome her insecurities and face any obstacle. Leos are the center of the universe, run by the sun. So, essentially, they light the fire for us to exist."

"Am I your reason to exist, Aundrea?"

"More than you'll ever know."

"What about these Pisces? What do they have to say?"

"Pisces is unique. They're ruled by Neptune and Jupiter, the ruler of seas and the king of Gods. Mixing those two together, you get some amazing and rare energy. We tend to be the most compassionate sign, wanting to take others' pain away. It's no wonder we'd need someone as strong as a Leo to lean on."

He's quiet for a moment, watching me. "Are you happy?"

"What do you mean?"

"With everything you've done in your life. Are you happy?"

"I couldn't have asked for a better life so far. I'm here, with you, a baby on the way, and about to start my dream career. I never thought all this was possible for me, so, yes, I am more than happy."

Taking a deep breath he releases my hand and rolls onto his back. "My nightmare … it always starts with me reading a letter from you. You say you'll be among the stars, watching and waiting. Do you think that's true?"

My chest squeezes. It seems just like something I would say.

I scoot closer to him and rest my hand on his cheek. His eyes close. "Absolutely, Parker. No matter where you are, if you stop and look up into the night sky and see a star twinkling, know that it's me giving you a wink back."

"I'm afraid."

"Of what?"

"What will be left if you're gone? I've run into Brandon twice recently and he looks so broken. I feel so bad for him. I *know* that's what trigged those dreams."

"You won't ever have to worry about that." I kiss the tip of his nose. "Think about what Dr. James said. I'm doing great. There's no need to worry."

"I was talking with Jason recently and he mentioned something about getting a will …" I tense immediately. "Aundrea, I'm not saying we need to plan for anything. It just got me thinking that with a baby on the way, we should be prepared. Make provisions for the practice, the house; I want *you* to be taken care of. I want our child to be looked after."

I process his words. I've never thought about getting a

will. I know Genna and Jason have one. I was there when they started talking about it and listened to them discuss it soon after I moved in with them. Genna was having one of her meltdowns about me and my treatment. About how she was tired of watching me in pain and wished she could take it all away. She said if anything happened to either of them, they should have something in place, so they agreed on getting a will.

"I think it's a good idea."

I hate having to discuss difficult topics like this, but they're necessary. Cancer or no cancer; cardiomyopathy or no cardiomyopathy. We need a will. We have assets to ensure and family to protect.

This is normal.

chapter

TWENTY

Aundrea

The end of August approaches and I have one week before I start my new job. I'm sad to leave For the Love of Paws, but excited for my next adventure.

Wendy's almost fifteen weeks along, now, and we're getting anxious for our eighteen-week ultrasound to find out the sex of the baby. Genna recommended a babymoon—something I'd never heard of before. It's basically an excuse to take a little vacation before the diaper-changing, scheduled feedings, and lack of sleep starts.

Parker is up earlier than normal for work, and he's moving quietly, trying not to wake me. Little does he know I've been awake almost all night thinking and enjoying a chance to watch him sleep peacefully.

I open my eyes as I hear him approach the bed.

"I'm sorry," he whispers, leaning down to kiss the top of my head goodbye.

"It's okay." He sits on the edge of the bed, so I scoot over to make room for him. "You're going to meet me at the lawyer's office, correct?" We're going to have our will drawn up by the same lawyer Jason and Genna used.

"Yes. At three?"

I nod.

He kisses my temple. My eyes drift closed again at the warm touch.

"Okay, I really have to get going before I ravish you right here and now. You're too damned tempting," he growls into my neck, playfully attacking me with nips and kisses.

I giggle. "Go, go!"

I'm grinning when he leaves.

I arrive early for our appointment, so I'm waiting for Parker when Jean calls.

"Hey, you!"

"Hi. Is this an okay time?"

"Yeah, I'm sitting outside the lawyer's office waiting for Parker."

"Oh, that's right. Sorry, I forgot your appointment was this afternoon."

"It's okay. I'm early."

We make small talk, then she asks, "When do we get to find out the sex of that baby?"

"Three weeks. I actually had a dream that the baby wouldn't uncross its legs so we didn't find out. I woke up telling Parker no matter what, we're shaking Wendy's stomach to make sure that baby cooperates." She giggles. "So … are you moving here?" I know she's not, but I like to keep pressing her. I have to listen to Kevin talk about it day in and day out at the clinic.

"No," she says, predictably. I let out an exaggerated sigh. "Hey now!"

"What?" I say innocently.

"Don't *what* me. Listen to me. My career is here and his is there. I love him, I do, but I'm not sure it's meant to be. We're both passionate about our work and neither of us wants to give up our career for the other. He's certain of that and, honestly, I am too. If it's meant to be, it's meant to be."

"You don't have to give up your career."

"No? We live two hours apart. Either he leaves the practice where he's partner, or I leave the place that could possibly be the best job in the world. Don't you see the problem there?"

"Not really. I mean, I see two stubborn people who love each other and are not together."

"So one of us should give up our job to be together?"

"If it means being together, it wouldn't even be a question for me."

"If you needed to relocate for Parker, would you? Now that you've found what you proclaim to be your dream job."

"In a second. There's only one Parker and many other jobs." She doesn't speak. I know she's contemplating my words. "You there?"

"Yeah. I hate it when you say shit like that."

"Like what?"

"The truth."

I laugh into the phone.

When Parker arrives I tell Jean I'll call her later.

"Hey!" I smile at him.

"Hey back."

He takes my hand and we walk into the office.

Michael, the lawyer, doesn't waste any time getting into it. Once we've covered most things, he brings up the baby and our frozen embryos.

"What do you want to do with the embryos?" he asks.

"Excuse me?" Parker looks at him, bemused.

"Did you write them into your contract with the agency?"

We shake our heads.

"Maybe you should donate them?" he suggests before continuing. "You'll want to make sure they're secure so in the event something does happen, a family member won't be able to go after the widower for the rights."

Would our families really do that? "I don't think my family would do that." I look at Parker and correct myself. "I don't think *our* families would."

"With all due respect Aundrea, you'd be surprised. If something happened to you, you'd want to make sure Parker has full custody of them, or … donate them."

Parker opens his mouth, but I cut in. "If something

happens to *either* of us, I'd like them to be property of the widower. In the event of a divorce, or if we both die, then they should be donated to Circle of Life."

"Parker?" Michael asks.

He looks at me with amazement. I can see he's proud of me for taking control of the conversation. "I completely agree."

"Good. Now, as for your unborn child. In the event of both of your deaths, who would you like to appoint as legal guardian?"

"Genna," we say together. That's never been a question. We couldn't think of a better person to look after our child … or children.

~℃ ℃~

Parker's ringing phone wakes me from a dead sleep. He doesn't move so I nudge him.

"Parker, your phone." It goes silent, but mine starts a moment later. I don't recognize the number, but answer groggily. "Hello?"

Someone clears their throat, then an unfamiliar voice says, "Hello, I'm sorry to disturb you in the middle of the night, but I'm looking for an Aundrea Jackson?"

"This is she."

"My name is Tonya, one of the nurses at Minneapolis Medical Center."

I sit up fast and my head spins.

"Yes?"

My anticipation grows stronger with each hammering beat of my heart.

"I'm calling on behalf of Mr. Henderson. He's requesting your presence."

Wendy. My heart sinks. "My presence? For what?"

Parker rolls over then, opening an eye.

"I'm sorry, but I'm not at liberty to say."

"What do you mean you're not at liberty to say? You're

the one calling here asking me to come to the hospital and you can't tell me why?"

Parker sits up then, taking the phone out of my hand.

"Who is this? What's going on?" *Fuck.*

I look at him, worried, but he holds his hand up.

"What do you mean you can't tell me? Fuck HIPAA! Put Ron on the phone. I need to make sure she's okay. Is she okay?"

He grows angrier, hanging the phone up.

"Parker?" I feel sick and I'm pretty sure I'm going to vomit.

"God damn it!" he screams as he throws the phone across the room. It shatters in an explosion of metal and plastic.

I begin to tremble.

Parker jumps out of bed and then doubles over.

"Parker!"

I run over to him. He's choking. "It's okay, babe. Breathe. Deep breaths in and out. That's it, in and out." My words come out smooth as I him take deep breaths. "Now, I need you to tell me what's going on."

His eyes flash to mine and I feel the blood drain from my face.

"Wendy."

chapter TWENTY-ONE

Aundrea

I'm not sure what's wrong with me, but I'm certain what I'm feeling isn't right. It's like sand is dripping down, clogging my throat.

Parker moves and speaks quickly. "We have to leave. The nurse won't tell me what's going on, but Wendy's been in some sort of accident."

"Oh, God," I choke out, covering my mouth. I pull on my shirt and tug at the neckline, trying to relieve the sensation that I'm choking. "What did the nurse say exactly?"

"She said nothing, Aundrea. That's the fucking problem! And Ron asked we be there, so we have to move. Now!" he snaps. I know he doesn't mean to, but he does.

"Parker, I'm scared." Every single terrible feeling I can imagine is coursing through me. I want to think positive, but I can't push through the fear no matter how hard I try.

"Aundrea, I need you to be strong right now. We need to leave."

I rush to grab clothes, as does Parker. I don't think we've ever moved so quickly in our lives.

If ever there was a time I didn't mind Parker's speeding habit, this is it. Now, he can't go fast enough for me. Since my phone is in pieces on our bedroom floor, I use Parker's to try and call Wendy's landline. I don't know who I'll get, maybe a family member watching their kids? Someone who can let me know what's going on. No one answers.

I try again. Then I try Ron's cell number. When he doesn't answer I try one more time.

Then one more, just in case.

Still no answer.

"Where the fuck is everyone?" I yell, pounding the dashboard in frustration.

Parker doesn't answer. I glance his way. I haven't looked at him since we got in the car, too afraid to meet his eyes. To see the hurt and worry there. His jaw is tight, his eyes wide with concentration, and he's white knuckling the steering wheel. Its then that I also notice our speed: a hundred miles an hour.

"Uh, Parker?"

No response.

"Parker."

No response.

"Parker!"

"What?" His voice slices through me.

"I understand we want to get there as quickly as we can, but we can't get there if we're hurt along the way."

He looks at the speedometer.

He lets off the gas just a little.

We don't speak for the duration of the ride. I do take his hand, though, needing to feel his touch. If ever I've needed him, it's now. My head hurts so much it feels like it's going to explode. It's the worst pain I've ever experienced, and that is saying a lot.

If I thought I knew what death felt like after chemo, I was wrong. So wrong. Because this feeling right now? This is death. The burning feeling, as if my whole body is breaking and being pulled every which way. It's the worst kind of pain I've ever had to endure as I think about all the worst-case scenarios that are speeding through my mind.

If anything has happened to our unborn child I don't think I'll ever recover. Our baby's life hasn't even truly begun; I can't fathom losing him or her before we even get the chance to meet.

Two hours has never felt so long in all my life. I feel like my skin is on fire and roll down the window to cool off, but it doesn't help.

"Aundrea, it's going to be okay. We need to have hope."

Hope. It's a word I've become familiar with.

The hospital lights blind me. All I see are the big red letters that spell EMERGENCY. Suddenly, my anxiety is unbearable. The moment I walk through those doors, my life could be changed forever.

Parker pulls into the ramp by the emergency room and takes the first spot he can find. We run to the entrance.

I'm not sure where we're going, and a small fraction of me isn't sure I want to find it yet. I'm scared. Terrified of what's to come. I say a silent prayer: *I want this baby more than anything. Don't take that away, please.*

Parker asks directions and we run, hand in hand, through the empty halls.

I hate the smell of hospitals. They all smell the same.

Like illness.

Stale death.

And they're always so bright. Like it's trying to convince us that an angel is there to save those who come through its doors.

I pray for an angel right now.

Parker runs to the emergency check-in desk, demanding to know where Wendy is. I can tell the nurse is freaked out. She keeps asking him to calm down. Parker's voice begins to rise and heads turn our way. I've never seen him like this. Then again, I've never had a reason to.

I scan the crowd and finally see Ron. "Aundrea!"

Parker's head snaps toward Ron's voice. Banging his hand on the counter, he pushes himself off. We meet halfway.

"Where is she?"

"Is the baby okay?"

"What's going on?"

"What happened?"

Ron can't get a word in. He gestures for us to stop.

I cling to Parker's arm, bracing myself for the worst. Worse than hearing my cancer is back. Worse than learning that my heart condition has gotten worse. Worse than being told a friend has died.

I close my eyes tightly, waiting—bracing myself.

"She's in surgery. She got into an accident on the freeway. Someone changing lanes wasn't paying attention and sideswiped the car. She got pushed into the guardrail."

I fall against Parker. *Surgery.*

"And the baby?" Parker pleads.

"As far as I know, the baby is okay. They said she fractured her arm pretty bad and they had to put her under to put in a plate. The surgeon told me they'd have the best team in there monitoring the baby. Didn't the nurse tell you this?" he looks really confused.

The baby is okay. Tears stream down my cheeks.

"No," Parker's voice cracks. "She wouldn't tell me anything. Something about HIPAA."

"Shit," Ron mumbles under his breath. "I told her to call and let you know what was going on and that the doctors said the baby was okay. I had to fill out paperwork and answer a bunch of questions from the staff, so I couldn't call. She came over once I was done and said she made the call, so I didn't think about it again. Hell, I'm sorry. I should have just called."

"It's not your fault," Parker says, patting his shoulder.

"I tried to call you," I squeak out.

Ron looks over to me, apologetically and takes out his phone. "Shit, I'm so sorry."

"It's okay. What's important is she's okay."

I see the tears forming in his eyes. "Yes."

We sit down and wait for an update on Wendy. On the baby. But no one comes.

Thirty minutes pass.

Then an hour.

I'm sipping my second cup of nasty, too-strong coffee when someone finally comes.

"Mr. Henderson?"

"That's me."

We all stand, anxious to hear the news.

"I'm Dr. Jenson." They shake hands and he looks over at us. "Is there somewhere we can talk in private?"

"Actually, these are the parents of the baby."

He nods. "Okay. Well, Wendy has suffered a serious compound fracture to her left arm. I've set it using a permanent plate. She may have some permanent nerve damage, but we won't know for sure until the cast comes off. Wendy's also suffered a number of bumps and bruises, including a fractured rib. Other than that, though, she was remarkably lucky. Neither car was going very fast, which I'm certain is what saved her."

"And the baby?" I ask, hopeful.

"The baby is doing fine." I sigh in relief, falling against Parker. He holds onto me, squeezing, letting me know he's right here. "There were no signs of distress when she was brought in, nor any during surgery. We had a team in there monitoring them the entire time. We'll keep Wendy a few days to make sure everything is okay with the baby but, so far, there are no signs of any complications."

"Thank God," I cry.

"The nurse is about to take her back for an ultrasound. Would you like to be there, too?"

We both nod, unable to speak, and follow Ron and the doctor. I know Ron must be anxious to see his wife.

My life isn't just mine anymore; I'm also living for someone else. I've been *so* focused on what will happen if I'm gone—on how those around me will respond and live—that I've never stopped to think how I'd feel if my child leaves *me*.

Wendy's sleeping when we enter the room. Her face is a little bruised and her arm is in a cast. Ron goes to her side and kisses her. I start to cry when I see her stomach through the blankets. Parker pulls me into a hug, letting me cry into his chest.

"I was so scared. So scared that we were going to be saying goodbye to someone we've never even met."

"Me too."

I'm shaking and Parker pulls me tighter against him.

"It's okay, babe. I got you. Let it out. Let it all out. They're okay. Shh."

"Hi, guys," Wendy's scratchy voice announces that she's awake.

"Hi," I say, stepping out of Parkers hold and closer to her. "Are you okay?"

She smiles. "I've been better. I'm so sorry." She starts to cry. "The last thing I want to do is to put your child in harm's way. I vowed to protect this baby. I'm so sorry!"

"We know you wouldn't do anything to harm the baby. That accident wasn't your fault," Parker reassures.

"I can't imagine what you two must have gone through."

"What matters right now is that you both are okay," I say, wrapping my arms around her.

The nurse comes in with the monitor. "Shall we take a peek at the little peanut?"

We nod and smile. Ron steps to the side, giving us more room.

One second I'm looking at a blank screen and the next I'm looking at a tiny human moving its hands and kicking its legs.

My heart stops. Literally, I can't feel it beating. "Holy shit." I'm in shock. I didn't know what to expect. I've seen ultrasounds on TV, and pictures, but to see my baby—*our* baby—in person, and moving … it's absolutely one of the most beautiful and rewarding things I've ever seen. Watching a stomach grow is one thing, but to actually see something you've created move is almost surreal.

"Wow," I breathe, squeezing Parker and Wendy's hands. The nurse moves about, taking measurements and explaining everything she's doing.

"Mr. and Mrs. Jackson you have one strong and healthy baby." My eyes mist over again. I watch the numbers bounce: 156, 158, 155, 160. *Strong*. That's what our baby is.

"Pretty cool, isn't it?" Wendy speaks, looking between us and the screen.

"Amazing," we say together.

"I'll print photos for you also," the nurse offers.

"Thank you!"

"Did you want to find out the sex?"

"Can you?" I ask.

"Fourteen weeks is the earliest. Wendy's almost fifteen, so we could take a look, if you'd like."

"Yes," Parker answers, swallowing.

I stare at our baby. I've been so anxious to know, but now I'm not so sure.

"Aundrea? You want to know, right?"

"I don't think so."

"You don't?"

I shake my head.

"But you hate surprises," he says.

I told him once that I hated them because, for me, they were never good. Parker's made it a point to give me as many happy ones as he can, though, in an attempt to change my mind.

"I used to. But I'm making new memories. I want to be surprised."

"Then let's be surprised." He grins at me and the nurse nods. Wendy tears up watching us.

The nurse finishes and leaves us alone. Wendy starts to drift in and out of sleep. I reach for Parker's hand. I take our clasped hands and place them on top of the covers, over Wendy's growing belly. Ron watches, but he remains quiet.

"No matter what our fears are, or what happens in the future, this"—I gesture to her stomach—"is what's left of us, Parker. He or she is a part of us, and no amount of fear will ever take that away. I will always be around, living through our child. And so will you."

A tear slides down his cheek. Leaning over Wendy's sleeping form, he kisses my forehead, lingering longer than normal. With a loud sigh, he releases me, and I look into his sad yet hopeful eyes.

"This baby is what's left of us," he repeats.

"Yes."

"What's left of you."

"And you. No matter what."

He holds my gaze, tears falling freely from both our eyes.

"I hope he has your eyes."

"I hope *her* eyes match your Caribbean blue." We both laugh lightly.

My past shaped me into the person I am today. I've been given the gift of life: mine, Parker's, and our child's.

I'm grateful for everything, including my fear. Sometimes we need those reminders to be fully awake.

To really see life.

EPILOGUE

Parker

Six months later

I wake up to the sound of Aundrea's phone vibrating on the nightstand. It gets louder only to stop and start back up again. Tossing and turning, I will the noise to stop.

The room goes quiet, aside from the sound of her peaceful breathing next to me. Squinting, I open my eyes. A little before 6:30. *Fuck, it's early.*

Aundrea's hand curls into my side, the other resting on my waist. I smile at the warmth I feel coming off of her. Letting out an exhausted sigh, I rub the sleep from my eyes and turn around to take in my beautiful wife, who is sleeping soundly. Rubbing her back, I remember the first time I held her in my arms: the night we met. I didn't want her to go, but I was afraid if I opened my mouth something idiotic would come out. So, instead, I did the gentlemanly thing. I covered her up with a blanket and wrapped her in my arms. It was never a one-night stand to me.

The buzzing stars back up again, but this time it's coming from my phone. *Who the hell is calling this early?*

Sliding away from Aundrea, I reach blindly for my

phone, then answer quickly when I see that it's Wendy.

"Parker! I'm sorry to keep calling, but it's time."

"Time?" I look at the time, not registering what she's saying.

"The baby. It's time for the baby!"

"Shit! Okay, we're on our way. Do we have time?"

She laughs. "Yes, my contractions are only five minutes apart. We're heading to the hospital as soon as they hit three minutes."

I practically fall out of bed, twisting myself in our sheets.

"Parker?" Aundrea sits up.

"Wendy called. It's time."

"Time?"

"Yes."

I flash her a grin and she runs over to me with the biggest smile on her face, any sleepiness obliterated by excitement.

I pick her up and pull her into a hug.

She kisses me once, then again.

"Oh, my God! It's time!" she says over and over again.

Aundrea and I rush through the hospital. I'm practically dragging her on her toes, trying to help her keep up. We pass a security guard and run up the stairs. I expect Wendy to be in the back triage area, but when I give the nurse her name, we're told she's already in a room.

Aundrea starts asking a bunch of questions. Her voice is calm, but her body language is anything but. She keeps running a hand through her hair and the normally bright hazel eyes that I love so much are clouded, looking everywhere.

A nurse walks us to the room.

"Wendy, I have two people who seem eager to see you."

Wendy is sitting on the side of the bed, her face scrunched, her hands on her stomach. Ron is standing behind her, rubbing her back and shoulders. Wendy requested in the contract that he be present for the birth and of course we agreed. Hell, I can use the extra testosterone in the room at a time like this.

"Hey, guys," she groans through clenched teeth.

I step further into the room and Aundrea moves right in front of Wendy and kneeling down, asks if she needs anything.

She shakes her head. After a few passing seconds, her breathing calms. She sits up taller, smiling. "Sorry. Worst time to enter." She chuckles.

"How far apart are the contractions?" Aundrea asks.

"Two minutes. It's moving quickly, but the baby is still a little high. I'm dilated to four centimeters and I've asked for an epidural."

"Good, drugs are good," I speak up. I'm not opposed to any painkillers that can help Wendy. We left that up to her in our contract. Aundrea and I only wanted what would make her comfortable.

"The contractions have been brutal, but they aren't lasting very long," Wendy says.

I read somewhere that the pain of giving birth feels like breaking twenty bones at one time. I'm immensely thankful that someone is willing to endure that kind of pain to give someone else the gift of life. Watching Wendy's contractions breaks me. It feels like someone is ripping out a piece of me.

When another contraction comes, Aundrea takes her hand, coaching her through it. It makes me so proud to watch her take charge like that. Ron doesn't say much, giving this moment to us, but he keeps his hand on Wendy's back, gently rubbing the whole time.

When the epidural finally arrives, we share the same look of relief. "One cocktail coming right up," the anesthesiologist jokes.

Wendy sits on the edge of the bed and bends forward, clutching a pillow. We're asked to stand off to the side. When a needle the size of my foot gets pulled out, Aundrea closes her eyes.

"That looks like the needle used for my bone marrow

transplant," she says shakily.

I pull her into my side. "This isn't the same thing, babe."

"I know, but I wish I could take it all away for her." I rub my hand along her lower back, soothing her.

"All right, you'll feel a little pressure here and then warmth from your waist down. You may feel tingling in your legs and toes," the anesthesiologist says to Wendy. "Okay, it's all done. I'm just going to tape this in place. It will take about thirty minutes until you feel the full effect."

Aundrea helps Wendy get comfortable again. The nurse readjusts the straps that help monitor the baby's heartbeat and Wendy's contractions, then Aundrea and I step out while she puts in a catheter. We're both more than happy to oblige.

"Is there a place to get something to drink?" I ask one of the nurses.

"Yes. There's a vending machine in the waiting room and the cafeteria is in the basement."

"How are you doing?" I ask Aundrea as we walk to the vending machine.

"Good. Nervous. Excited."

"Me too. I can't believe it's finally here." All I want is to be a good father and give my children everything they need. I want nothing but the best for them. I want Wendy to have a safe and easy delivery, and us to welcome a healthy baby. I stop in the middle of the hallway, and kiss Aundrea. I put my hands on top of hers, rubbing my thumbs gently along her cold fingers.

"I love you."

"I love you more, handsome."

"You and me. Don't forget that."

After getting water, we walk back to Wendy. She's almost asleep when we enter. I try not to make a sound, but I accidentally squeeze the plastic bottle and the crunching sound startles Wendy.

"I'm so sorry," I say quietly.

"Don't worry about it. You're okay."

"Do you need anything?"

"I can only have ice chips going forward, so maybe some of those?"

"Sure, I'll go find some."

I give Aundrea a wink as I pass by. As I leave the room, I hear Wendy say, "You two are so cute." I stop, waiting for Aundrea's reply. I can almost sense the blush creeping over her face.

"Thank you."

"I love that he winks at you."

"Me too."

I smile and walk away. I'll have to remember to wink more often.

When I approach the room, Aundrea's voice echoes out into the hallway.

"Cocky."

"Cocky?" I ask, raising an eyebrow. "Who's cocky?" Aundrea gives Wendy an "I told you so look" which makes me laugh. "I *knew* you were talking about me while I was gone."

Wendy looks at Aundrea and she shakes her head, smirking. "We don't *always* talk about you, Parker."

"Nonsense. I'm always on your mind."

～♂ ♀～

Three hours later, the nurse comes into the room. "I'm going to do an exam, okay?"

"Yeah." Wendy looks exhausted and I feel bad there isn't more I can do for her. I stand up to give the nurse more room, glancing at Aundrea.

"Well, you're at ten and the baby's head is right here! I'm going to go page the doctor. Looks like someone will be pushing any minute."

My heart speeds up. Aundrea takes my hand and I look over to her. "Ready, handsome?"

"More than ready." I've been waiting for this moment.

To hold our baby in my arms.

I give her a kiss, then one more for good measure.

Two nurses return, one pushing a small table with the baby bed under a large light.

When the doctor comes in, he's all smiles. "Are we ready to meet the little one?"

"You have no idea," we say together.

Aundrea and I stand on one side of Wendy and Ron stands on the other, taking her hand. Aundrea rubs her arm, speaking words of encouragement.

The nurse coaches Wendy on a couple practice pushes. I'm not sure what a practice push is exactly. It's either you're pushing, or you're not. When she tells her she's doing a great job, I do the same.

Wendy wasn't lying when she said she had fast deliveries. After only two full sets of pushes the doctor tells her she's starting to crown.

"I-is it supposed to look like that?" Aundrea asks with surprise. It takes everything in me not laugh. Everyone else does.

"Yes, it's normal," the doctor says.

She looks at me and smiles embarrassedly. "Uh, just checking." Looking up at Wendy, she gives her an encouraging smile. "You're doing great!"

Wendy barely gets out a chuckle before she goes back to pushing, bearing all her weight down and squeezing my hand.

"Holy, shit." I can't be sure if I say that in my head or out loud, but I say it again a couple more times.

"Okay, Wendy. One more really big push," the doctor instructs.

I look over at Aundrea who's holding onto Wendy's leg like it's her job. She looks so beautiful right now, coaching the woman who is about to welcome our child into the world.

Aundrea senses me watching and looks over. I give her a wink and rub her back. It's a small gesture, but it's something to let her know that I'm here with her.

This is our moment.

Wendy pushes with a groan, and I see a baby. All the air is sucked out of my lungs and everything begins to happen so fast. Words are being said, small body parts are becoming more visible, and, before I know it, a baby is being placed on Wendy's chest.

A nurse begins cleaning the little one off.

"Dad, would you like to cut your little boy's cord?"

A boy!

"Yes. Yes, I would." Before I release Aundrea, I whisper, "It's a boy."

Watching our child be born is more than magical. It's beautiful. We're welcoming him into the world. This is a feeling of unconditional love I'll never forget. I want to stay lost in this moment with Aundrea forever as I stare at our baby.

I take the scissors from the doctor and tears instantly sting my eyes as I cut the cord. After it's done, the nurse takes our little man away to get cleaned and weighed.

"Seven pounds, four ounces. Twenty inches," the nurse says. She wraps the baby and hands him to Aundrea. When our son is in her arms, Aundrea says, "Seeing you is worth every minute it took to get you to us. I don't know how I ever made it through life before you." She stops and looks over at me. "He's a part of us, Parker, and he's more beautiful and perfect than I could have ever imagined."

I stand next to her, looking down at our baby boy. So tiny and small. Two dark eyes stare up at us. I read babies can't see very far when they're first born, so I get real close to his face.

"Hi, Mason. I'm your daddy. This is your mommy and we love you so much." I bend down giving our baby a tiny kiss. "*I* love you so much."

"I can't believe this. He's so beautiful," Aundrea whispers.

I wrap an arm around her waist. "We did it."

"We did it," she repeats.

Looking back down at Mason I smile. I just got this

beautiful baby and I already know I'll wake up every morning vowing to do anything in this world to protect him.

I already can't live without him.

～ ⊙ ～

It's been three days since we brought Mason home and in those three days our life has changed so much. My life is no longer mine. It's Mason's. Everything we do is for him, and neither of us would have it any other way.

"Shh, it's okay. I know what it's like to not want to sleep at night, but believe me when I tell you that there is nothing to be afraid of. A little wet diaper isn't anything to get worked up about." I finish changing his diaper, wrapping him back up so he's nice and warm before putting him back in his crib.

In our room, Aundrea's sitting in bed with the lamp on.

"You're awake?"

She points to the monitor and I smile as I crawl back into bed, getting comfortable.

"Parker?"

"Hmm?"

"Thank you."

"For what?"

"For giving me the best gift in the world."

"Thank you for saying yes."

One word has changed my life. Her saying yes to going home with me the night we met, yes to our first date, yes to marrying me, and, lastly, yes to having a child.

～ ⊙ ～

The next morning I'm making coffee when Aundrea joins me in the kitchen.

"What are you so happy about this morning?" she asks, resting her head on my shoulder.

"You opened your eyes."

"Huh?"

"In my dream." She looks over at me, perplexed. "It

started out how it has before, but then … you opened your eyes, Aundrea. It changed."

She kisses my lips.

I take a deep breath and let it out slowly. I knew this day would come. Aundrea and Mason are my heart. And sometimes your heart and mind are equal partners. She's taught me to conquer my own fear and, because of that, for the first time, I was able to watch my wife open her eyes, changing what was once a nightmare into something bright.

I wrap my arms around her and hold on tight. I take in her pear and honey scent and smile. This is my life.

Soft cries interrupt our embrace. "I'll go," she whispers against my lips.

The doorbell rings and people start piling in.

Both sets of parents come up from downstairs. Mine flew in two days ago to see their grandson and help out for a week and Aundrea's came up the night Mason was born.

"Hey guys, come on in."

Shannon walks in first, followed by Kevin and Jean who have their arms around each other. Jason, Genna, and Hannah arrive shortly before ten. Donna and Genna start making brunch right away, which is when Wendy arrives with her family. We wanted to have all our family and friends with us to welcome Mason. Each person here has played a role in getting him into our arms. We couldn't have done it without their support.

When everyone is gathered in the kitchen, I make a toast. "I want to thank everyone for coming here this morning and spending the day with us. Aundrea and I especially want to thank Wendy." I look over at Wendy. "Wendy, you have given us something that we'll forever be thankful for. You've become a part of our family and we want you to know you're always welcome."

I hand her a small white box.

"You didn't have to get me something, you guys," she says.

"We wanted to," Aundrea says.

"Think of it as a belated push present."

Aundrea opens her mouth in shock. Wendy laughs.

"Parker, how do you know about push presents?" Genna presses.

"I know a thing or two."

Wendy opens the box to find a picture frame. On one side is a photo of Wendy, me, and Aundrea holding Mason just hours after he was born. The other side of the frame is engraved, "I'm here because of you."

Wendy starts to cry. "Wow, this is the best gift. I don't know what to say. Thank you."

"No, thank you. Like Parker said, we couldn't have done this without you. I will forever be grateful for what you've given us."

Wendy passes the frame around. When Genna holds it, she gazes at it intently. "I never would have thought that my little sister would marry a man I introduced her to and go on to have a baby. Miracles do happen."

Jean and Shannon both burst out laughing at the same time.

"You didn't introduce them," Jean says, eyes filling with tears she's laughing so hard.

"What are you talking about?" Genna looks at us, confused.

"You mean you have no idea? To this day?" Shannon asks.

"No idea about what?"

Everyone turns to us.

I can only manage a shrug.

Aundrea's cheeks flush a deep red.

It's not that we've kept how we met a secret. People just assumed we met through For the Love of Paws and we've never found it important to correct them.

"You mean … you two met before the night at our house?" Genna interrogates.

"Uhh …" Aundrea looks uncomfortable and I find it absolutely adorable.

"Yes," I answer for both of us. The room goes silent. I swear you could hear a pin drop. "Honestly, I'm surprised it never came out sooner."

"How?" Genna looks between the two of us.

Both sets of parents look at each other. My mom speaks up. "I think we'll take the kids in the living room." Jay takes Hannah from Jason and they all exit.

I chuckle at their embarrassment. We have smart parents. I'm pretty confident they've figured out exactly how we met.

I start to speak, but Aundrea cuts in. I love when she takes charge. "We met at Max's Bar the night Jean came to visit."

I know the moment the light bulb goes on in Genna's head because her eyes get wide. "Did you two …?"

"Oh, hell," Jean laughs out. "They did more than hook up. Those two were all over each other that night, grinding and making out by the bathrooms. She was too chicken to leave, but finally grew some tits and went home with him."

"*She's* the girl you left with?" Kevin says loudly, in realization.

I nod.

"Damn." He laughs.

"So, that night at our house," Jason begins, "the two of you already knew each other."

"Yes," Aundrea confirms.

"How long were you two hooking up before you announced that you were dating?" Genna asks, hands on hips. I can't tell if she's upset because she didn't know or because she wasn't the one who actually introduced us.

"We weren't," Aundrea answers.

"Well, unless you count the make out session at the clinic right before you started," I counter.

Aundrea swats my chest playfully and I laugh.

"Oh, come on guys! She turned me down countless times. I had to work for it—hard. I mean, it took me a long time just to get her to agree to go on a darn date with me to the hockey game."

"That wasn't a date," Aundrea insists.

"Babe, call it what you will. It was a date."

"I can't believe I was so blind," Genna says.

"No shit; well played, guys," Jason adds. He's smiling. "No wonder you were so shocked to see him in our living room that night. Here I thought you were mesmerized by his good looks when, really, it's just a total nightmare to see your one-night stand in your sister's living room. Damn. That's quite funny, really, looking back." He laughs harder.

"You." Genna shakes her head at Aundrea. "I never would have thought you had it in you, sister."

Aundrea laughs, then she turns serious as she looks at me. "I never thought my Mr. One Night Stand would become my future."

I pull her close. "And I'm not going anywhere."

"Speaking of which," Jean announces, pulling our attention back. She steps close to Kevin and takes his hand. "Neither am I."

"What do you mean?" Aundrea asks.

"I'm moving to Rochester."

"You are?" Aundrea's face lights up and she practically slams into Jean as she pulls her into a hug.

Jean just shakes her head.

I knew she and Kevin would figure it out.

Eventually, we all join the parents in the living room. Looking around, though, I don't see Aundrea. I finally find her in the basement, gathering food from our snack bar.

"Hey, do you need any help?"

"No, thanks, I got it." She shoots me the smile that hits me like a bolt of lightning. I take the snack bowls out of her hand.

"What?"

"I bought you something."

"You didn't need to get me anything."

"Yes, I did." I pull a tiny gold locket from my pocket.

Aundrea takes it, opening the small heart. Inside is a photo of me, holding Mason. The locket reads, "We're here because of you."

"Parker," she exhales.

"You once told me that I have to surround myself with light and give it to others. I can only hope to give you and Mason as much light as you've given me."

"Parker." She pulls me into her arms, hugging me as tight as she can. "How did I get so lucky?"

"I ask myself the same thing every day."

We've said those words to each other before, but they're true. I'm still amazed this woman chose me.

"I love you, Aundrea."

"I love you more, handsome."

"If you say so." I smile.

Some people search their entire lives for that one person they can't live without; who is their other half in every way possible.

Aundrea is mine.

We're intertwined.

For life.

Acknowledgments

It's hard to believe I'm here again, writing my mini novella of thanks for my second novel. In *What's Left of Me* I started out the acknowledgements thanking those that inspired me to sit down and write Parker and Aundrea's story. I believe it's only fair I start these out in the same manner. I owe this book to YOU, the reader. I don't believe thank you will ever be enough, but with everything inside of me thank you from the bottom of my heart. I'll never forget the countless emails, tweets, Facebook messages and posts, asking for more Parker and Aundrea. Your love for these characters brought this story to life. I never imagined any other story for them. So, once again, thank you for your constant support.

My love, my life, my friend: You're one of my biggest supporters and make me a better person. You listen when I need to talk out an idea and never mind brainstorming with me. Thank you for believing in me and never letting me give up. I love you.

My two amazing little boys: The dedication says it all.

My wonderful parents: You're there for me when I need to talk about everything in the "book world" and are my biggest fans. Thank you for coming to signings with me, telling everyone you know about my books and believing in me. You'll never understand what you two mean to me.

Beth Suit: You read this book in its rawest form and never stopped believing in it. Thank you for all your advice and suggestions on making Parker and Aundrea's story all the better.

Con Copon and Beth Simkanin: You two were the first to read this book, and I'll be forever thankful for all the love and advice that was given. You two have been by me from the very beginning and I couldn't imagine my life without either of you.

Christine Borgford: I've said this to you countless times, but I'll say it again: Thank you! Thank you for being there for me when I needed to talk about this story, cheering me on, and loving these characters just as much as I do. Thank you for pushing me and telling me this story needed to be told. Your advice has helped shape this into a better story.

Brooke Page: You've read this book countless times and no matter the draft, you've loved it. You told me readers needed this book and no matter what, I needed to stay true to myself and these characters. No matter what you say, you're an amazing beta and I'm so lucky you took the time to read this story. Thank you for your constant advice and support. I'm lucky to call you a friend.

Amy Marie: You have a heart of gold and are an amazing friend, author, and beta. Thank you for taking the time to read Parker and Aundrea's story in the very early stages, answering all my questions, and being in my corner. I adore you!

Nicky Olson: You're always there to answer my medical questions, or correct me when I think I'm right. Thank you for all your support.

Shannon Smith and Genna Bichler: Thank you for standing by me and listening to all my crazy ideas and stories. You're always standing behind me, cheering me 110%.

Samien Newcomb: Even though you don't like stories about pregnancy, you took a chance on me and came out cheering! Your advice and constant support mean the world to me. Thank you for being an awesome beta!

Christine Estevez: You came into my life and now I don't ever want you to leave! You were there for me when I needed it and were nothing but honest. Thank you for all your advice and suggestions when it came to this book. You knew just where to add "more" and where to cut back. Thank you!

Jessica Guerrero: Thank you for beta reading this book. Your constant updates had me cheering from the roof tops. From the first few pages you totally got and understood Aundrea the way I hoped a reader would. You've believed in me and this story from the beginning and I'm so thankful for your feedback. You're an amazing woman and I'm lucky to call you a friend.

Tabby Coots: You, my friend, have the biggest heart and are a huge inspiration. Thank you loving and understanding these characters just as much as me. You understood my vision from the start and were one of the few to get a small preview of where this story was going. You continue to cheer me on and push me to be a better writer. Thank you!

Jennifer Roberts-Hall: You get me. The moment I started talking about this story you understood my vision and direction. You didn't let me steer from it and kept me on track. Thank you for working on *What's Left of Us* and loving these characters. True to your words, you didn't let me have one bad sex scene and even requested more! You're the queen of "trimming down" and I love you for it.

Rebecca Peters-Golden: I'd be lost without you. You have an amazing talent for turning the simplest of sentences into a work of art. Thank you for everything you have done with this book and correcting all my terrible grammar and spelling errors!

Regina Wamba: You're truly a gifted woman. When I saw this cover photo I knew it was Parker and Aundrea. It's as if you took this one photo with this book in mind. Thank you for always being patient and so kind.

Brandee Veltri with Brandee's Book Endings: You've stood by me from the very beginning and I couldn't be more thankful. Thank you for believing in me, listening to me talk out this story, and beta reading. Also, thank you for all your hard work with the cover reveal and blog tour. I appreciate everything you do so much! I'd be lost without your friendship.

Lisa Schilling Hintz with The Rock Stars of Romance: As always, thank you for your friendship and constant support. You're always in my corner, rooting me on and doing your best to get the word out for my stories. Thank you for all you've done for me and your promotional expertise!

My DAU girls -Trudy Stiles and Rebecca Shea: You ladies make everything brighter. I am so blessed to have met you. I look forward to our phone chats, group messages, and even texts. You're always there to give advice, listen to me talk about anything and everything that's going on in my life and are in my corner no matter what. Also, thank you for always being around to answer a question when in need. You both light up my life!

Giulie Kiessling and Tami Lee: You two women mean the world to me! Thank you for your continued support and believing in my work. You make each day better.

Polly Barreto: Meeting you at the E.L James book signing was fate. You're a true friend, supporter, and pusher. You pushed for me to write more Parker and Aundrea and no matter what, you believed in me and my writing. Thank you!

Lisa Pantano Kane: I'm still in shock by how much love you have for Parker and Aundrea. Since our first encounter you've been a huge supporter of me and I'll be forever thankful for your kind and loving friendship.

Steph Nuss: There is no amount of words for what your friendship and support have meant to me. Thank you for everything.

Nic Farrell: Your words of encouragement mean everything to me. You're always there to swoop in. Thank you for being such an amazing friend and support system.

Emmy Hamilton: You have an eye for detail. Thank you for taking one last look through on *What's Left of Us* and catching the things I missed!

To all the authors in my support group: Each and every single one of you inspires me to be a better writer. I'm still shocked I'm in this industry with you. There isn't a day that goes by that I'm not thankful for all the advice and support each of you have given me. From the bottom of my heart, thank you.

AL Jackson, Willow Aster, Kahlen Aymes and Sloan Johnson: You women have been a huge inspiration to me. You're all equally talented and have written some of my favorite books of all time. I'm still in awe to be among you in this amazing author world. Thank you for accepting me, befriending me, recommending and believing in my work.

To all the amazing women in my street team and the *What's Left of Me* (and soon to be *What's Left of Us*) reader group: I don't think thank you is enough for all you do, but thank you. I love interacting with each and every one of you. Your messages light up my day! Thank you for your continued support and loving Parker and Aundrea. Thank you for wanting more and believing in me!

To every single one of you bloggers, big or small: We're all in this together and I'd be nowhere without your support and love for reading. Each and every single one of you are valuable and I'm so thankful you've welcomed me into this world with open arms. Thank you for helping get this story out there, believing in me and my writing, and supporting my stories.

To whom ever I missed: I'm sorry, but please know it wasn't intentional. There are so many people I've come in contact with over the last few years and you all continue to amaze me with how welcoming you are: bloggers, authors, readers and friends. Thank you for everything.

About the Author

Amanda Maxlyn lives in Minnesota with her husband and two little boys. When she's not writing, she can be found outside with her family, or snuggled up with her Kindle, a glass of wine, and her fictional friends.

To stay updated on current information and upcoming novels make sure to subscribe to her blog at www.amandamaxlyn.com

Connect with Amanda via:

Facebook: https://www.facebook.com/AmandaMaxlynAuthor

Twitter: https://twitter.com/amandamaxlyn

CPSIA information can be obtained
at www.ICGtesting.com
Printed in the USA
LVOW13s1757011017
550766LV00012B/713/P